THE
BEACH COTTAGE

ALSO BY JOANNE DEMAIO

The Seaside Saga
Blue Jeans and Coffee Beans
The Denim Blue Sea
Beach Blues
Beach Breeze
The Beach Inn
Beach Bliss
Castaway Cottage
Night Beach
Little Beach Bungalow
Every Summer
Salt Air Secrets
Stony Point Summer
—And More Seaside Saga Books—

Summer Standalone Novels
True Blend
Whole Latte Life

Winter Novels
Eighteen Winters
First Flurries
Cardinal Cabin
Snow Deer and Cocoa Cheer
Snowflakes and Coffee Cakes

Novella
The Beach Cottage

the Beach Cottage

A NOVELLA

Joanne DeMaio

This is a work of fiction. Names, characters, places, and incidents are either the product of the author's imagination or are used fictitiously. Any resemblance to actual persons, living or dead, events, or locales is entirely coincidental.

No part of this book may be reproduced, or stored in a retrieval system, or transmitted in any form or by any means, electronic, mechanical, photocopying, recording, or otherwise, now known or hereinafter invented, without express written permission of the copyright owner.

Copyright © 2020 Joanne DeMaio
All rights reserved.

ISBN: 9798674725985

Joannedemaio.com

To Mary

*For telling me to write this story,
my way.*

one

"NOT TOO MUCH FARTHER," THE man driving says as he turns the car off the main drag. "The beach cottage is at the end of that dirt road there."

The woman beside him leans forward and looks closely out the windshield. She seems doubtful—as though not believing this dirt path winding through a forest will ever bring them to a beach.

"This is *it?*" she asks from the passenger seat. She lifts her tortoise-shell sunglasses to the top of her head. "Are you sure this is the right place, Mack? I mean, it's all woods and trees." She holds onto the door and looks out her window. Leafy branches brush close. A faded *Dead End* sign is nailed into the bark on one of those trees.

"Avery," Mack tells her. There's a casual look to him. He's been driving with his window down, so his dark hair is windblown. A shadow of whiskers covers his face, too. His left arm is crooked on that open window as he lightly holds the steering wheel. "I've been coming here every summer of my life. So that's thirty-four summers now. I think I know where my family's beach cottage is."

But every time they round a bend in the road, Avery deflates a little more. It's as though she expects each bend to open to a coastal vista. And to summer cottages. Instead, they only drive deeper into woods. Towering trees lining the roadside create a dark canopy in the midday sunlight. Dappled shadows fall on the dirt road as the car maneuvers each curve twisting left, or right, into some thick forest obscuring the summer day's lightness. There's another tree-mounted sign— this one black with red letters declaring, *No Trespassing*.

"It's just that I pictured our honeymoon different than … *this*," Avery softly explains. "I thought it would be more like an exclusive resort."

"And *I* thought we agreed. You wanted all the bells and whistles at our wedding. The photo booth. And ice sculpture. The choreographer we hired for the surprise wedding party dance. The deluxe lighting package. And did we really need miniature maracas for wedding favors?"

"You used them, didn't you, Mack Martinelli? On the dance floor?"

"Fair enough, I did. But let's also not forget your big three-oh birthday party last month—which put a huge dent in our budget."

"Hey, wait. I turned thirty, true. But I also made that girls' weekend Vermont birthday getaway my bachelorette party!"

The Beach Cottage

Mack glances over at Avery. "Regardless," he says, taking yet another dark curve along the wooded road. "Our sizable wedding budget trimmed the honeymoon budget to this." Mack nods toward the road.

"This." Avery tucks her sandy blonde hair behind an ear and sits back with a sigh—then leans away from the door when wayward underbrush sweeps against the car. "I guess I was hoping for something ... *more*. Especially since our honeymoon is just forty *minutes* from home. Never mind a tropical island, we're not even leaving Connecticut."

"Oh, believe me. It'll feel like we did. As soon as we get there."

They're quiet then. Their vehicle, a muscle car of some sort, purrs with a low rumble along the rutted dirt road. Clouds of dust rise around the car's tires. The forest blocking the sun keeps Avery and Mack in vague darkness. The only hint that it's actually daytime is the twittering birdsong.

Until suddenly they round one last curve in the road—and the world opens up.

There, on the left, an expansive lawn leads to an old painted house. Avery sits straighter as the forest-lined dirt road changes. The sky lightens now, too, up ahead. The more Mack drives, the more blue sky comes into view. And as the sky gets lighter, that sunshine falls on cottages. Not many, just a few shingled homes nestled on large manicured lawns. Manicured lawns with shady trees.

But the view beyond each shingled cottage is all that

matters. All that might get you to take a deep, slow breath. That view is obviously the draw of this place. The blue waters of Long Island Sound reach to a far horizon framed only by wisps of white clouds.

"Here we are," Mack says, turning into a driveway that's nothing more than packed-down lawn. Their black two-door coupe shifts over gentle heaves in the ground before coming to a stop. "And it's only Sunday, so we'll have a nice, long beach week."

In the bright sunlight, Avery drops her sunglasses back onto her face. Leaning low to look out Mack's window, she sees the cottage there. It's a rambling bungalow-style one-story, with a sloped roof. The weathered silver shingles look like they've been brushed with the very salt of the sea. Slate-blue trim frames paned windows. There are beach roses heavy with pink blossoms and green leaves climbing up a trellis beside one of those windows. On the side of the cottage, there's a deck. And in the front, a flower garden grows around a twisted driftwood log that's aged to shades of gray and copper.

"Your cottage is really pretty. But I don't know, Mack," Avery says as she opens the car door and gets out. Reaching into the back for her luggage, she looks over the seat at him. "At least we have a full itinerary planned, so we're not just sitting on sand chairs for seven days."

The Beach Cottage

"I'm famished!" Avery settles into her seat at the stately Old Lyme Inn that evening. She wears a cropped white blazer over a navy top and faded jeans. A chunky beaded gold necklace loops around her neck. "Unpacking gives me such an appetite, every time."

"The salt air does it for me," Mack muses. After cuffing the sleeves of his button-down, he picks up a menu. "Let's see what we want to eat."

They sit at a side table in the historic inn's dining room. Tall paned windows are trimmed in wide sage molding; soft evening sunlight shines on the white-oak floor; a bottle of wine is on their table. As they browse the menus, there's something more, too, in the hushed room. There's chatter, nervous chatter, coming from a few patrons. They're sitting on upholstered stools at the wooden bar just across the room.

Heard the governor might issue stay-at-home orders.
Trying to fight the pandemic.
Connecticut cases rising.
Hospitalizations up.
Virus spreading.
But shut down the whole state?
Things aren't looking too good.

With an ear tuned to the dire words, Mack and Avery occasionally look at each other over their menus until their waiter approaches.

"Evening, folks. What can I get you tonight?" he asks.

Mack motions to Avery.

"I'll have the ..." She drags a finger down the menu. "Lobster ravioli," she says with a nod. "And the house salad."

"Very good. And you, sir?"

"Filet mignon for me."

"How would you like that cooked?"

"Medium rare. With the baked potato, and ..." Mack sets down the menu, then motions the waiter closer. "Can I ask you something?"

"Absolutely."

"What's going on? The pandemic's gotten that serious?" Mack asks.

"It's all anyone's talking about these days." The waiter glances over at the bar customers. "Where've you been?"

"Out of the loop, apparently," Mack admits.

"We actually just got married. Yesterday," Avery says with a distracted glance at the bar, too.

"Well now. That explains it—you've been ... preoccupied?" their waiter asks.

"To say the least," Avery agrees. "Showers, parties. The rehearsal, *and* wedding. It's been a whirlwind. We just arrived today for our honeymoon."

"Congratulations, you two. So you're booked here at the inn?" The waiter flips his order pad closed.

"No. No, we just stopped in for dinner," Mack tells him. "Actually staying at Hatchett's Point, down the road a ways."

"Ah, nice place, right here in Old Lyme. So … you're not from around these parts?" the waiter asks.

"Oh, we are," Mack says. "Live just inland, outside of Hartford. Keeping the honeymoon local, though."

"You work local, too?"

"We do," Avery tells the waiter as she hands him back their menus. "I design the window displays for a nearby shopping plaza." She turns to Mack. "And my husband's family owns Martinelli Upholstering."

"That's a familiar name," the waiter says as he tucks their menus beneath an arm. "I've heard you do great work."

"Appreciate that," Mack tells him. "But right now, I'm worried about that pandemic more than anything else."

"I hear you. Scary stuff, especially if the state closes down." The waiter gives a slight salute as he heads toward the kitchen with their orders. "Hope you're well-stocked with supplies," he calls back over his shoulder.

―

By the time they get to the supermarket after dinner, the sun's gone down. Mack grabs a shopping cart and wheels it through the doors. But when they turn to the produce aisle, he stops.

"You should get another carriage," he tells Avery.

Avery comes up beside him and brushes her fingers across his whiskered jaw. "Are you sure? Maybe you're overreacting."

All Mack has to do is nod to the empty shelves. Only shreds of lettuce are left. And a few scattered tomatoes. A half-dozen zucchinis, which he grabs. Some berries and nectarines. "Get another carriage," he tells Avery again, his voice lower this time.

When she returns, they slowly walk up and down the aisles. The lighting is harsh at this nighttime hour. The shelves, half empty.

"This is so weird," Avery softly says, looking back over her shoulder. "Is this really happening? The way everything's picked over, and the way the store's so quiet, it's like the world's coming to an end."

Mack looks back, too. Then he keeps walking. He tosses in anything they might need. Some canned goods. Breads they can freeze. Avery fills her cart with paper products. She adds cleaning sprays and disposable gloves—what's left of them, anyway.

"Really?" Mack asks. "Disposable gloves?"

Avery nods toward two women wearing blue latex gloves while shopping. "I've never seen anything like this," she whispers in the oddly hushed store.

"Let's plan out for the week, then. We'll have to grab food for dinners. Maybe some hamburger patties. A chicken."

"But we have *reservations*. And at some of the nicest restaurants!" Avery insists from behind Mack. "Don't you think we'll be all set? And your family filled the fridge for us."

Mack watches an older couple hurry past. Their

steps are quick; the woman clutches a long list. "I don't know, Avery." He looks back at her pushing her carriage. "I'm getting a bad feeling about this. We're here, so it can't hurt to stock up."

Soon the groceries—readymade salads, salmon fillets, bakery rolls—are bagged and loaded into the car trunk. But driving back to the beach cottage, Avery and Mack say little. Instead, Mack tunes the radio to a local station. They listen to the latest news—hearing some imminence in the announcer's tone.

When Mack turns the car onto the long dirt road leading to the cottage, the forest seems more ominous than ever. Trees throw black shadows in the headlight illumination. A raccoon plods across the road. The car engine rumbles as the vehicle shifts and sways on heaves in the packed dirt. At one point, Avery snaps off the radio, then sits back and crosses her arms. The night presses against the car windows.

Finally, the cottages come into view. Beyond them, a heavy moon rises over Long Island Sound. It drops a swath of silver on the water. When Mack turns the car into their driveway, their beach cottage is so dark, it's barely visible. Every window is as black as the night.

Avery reaches over and squeezes Mack's arm. "*You didn't leave a light on?*" she whispers.

two

SOMETHING ABOUT THE EARLY LIGHT of day edging the curtains changes things. You can see it in the way the couple lounges in bed, beneath the sheets, Monday morning. Avery lies on her side. Mack moves closer, and from behind, wraps an arm around her.

"Good morning, Mrs. Martinelli," he says, then kisses the side of her head. A few moments later, he lifts the sheet and gets out of bed.

"While you're up, can you get my robe?" Avery's sleepy voice asks.

Mack lifts the short satin robe off the bed's white wrought-iron footboard. Standing there in his pajama bottoms, he lets the robe's fabric stroke the skin of her legs, her arms. "You sure you want it right now?"

"Mack!" Avery sits up and takes the robe, slipping it on over her chemise. "We're going out to breakfast, remember?"

Lifting his wrinkled tee off that same footboard,

Mack pulls the shirt over his head. Walking to the windows, he sweeps open the white curtains, which gets Avery to squint at the brilliant sunshine glinting off the expanse of Long Island Sound beyond.

"I'll put on coffee," Mack tells her as he kisses her again, and strokes her blonde hair. "You relax."

So Avery sits alone on the bed. She takes a few breaths of the salt air filling the room. When the cry of seagulls reaches her, she walks over to those windows. Outside, a large lawn slopes down to dune grasses, beyond which lies the sea. Looking rested and at ease, Avery simply stands there—taking it all in. The sound of distant waves can be heard, too. Over and over, they lap onshore.

In another moment, though, a different sound gets her to turn her head. Mack must've put on the TV in the other room. A news anchor's muffled voice drifts close. When Avery turns toward the doorway, Mack is standing there—his hair mussed, a coffee in hand.

"We're on lockdown," he says.

"What?"

"We're not going out to breakfast. The governor announced the lockdown first thing. Except for essential businesses, the entire state of Connecticut is shut down."

"But ... but *restaurants*?" Barefoot, Avery steps closer to Mack. "Aren't they essential? We have to eat."

"At home, apparently. Everything's closed, Avery. They showed a graph on TV. I guess the virus numbers are really spiking. Positive cases, up. Hospitalizations. Deaths. It's right at our doorstep now. And the governor's aim is to slow the spread of that virus and flatten the graph's curve." Mack sips from his coffee cup. "Stay-at-home orders have been issued."

"But this is our honeymoon!" Avery hurries back to the open window and looks out at the sunny morning. "I don't know," she quietly says then. "Maybe we should just leave." She squints over at Mack for a long second. "What's the point of looking out a window all week? It's like we're trapped here."

"No." He walks into the bedroom and sets his coffee on a painted dresser. "Not trapped. We're … hidden away. There's a difference. We're hidden away from the rest of the world."

"Either way, we're in isolation."

"With the love of your life."

"Mack. You know what I mean. I didn't plan to *sit* here for an *entire* week. That's not a honeymoon."

Mack walks closer and takes her hands in his. "Some people would stay in bed all week now, and love that honeymoon. With a sea breeze blowing in. My arm around your shoulders. Whiling away the days beneath cool sheets."

Avery takes a quick breath and walks to the nightstand, where she turns on her cell phone. Right away, it starts dinging with accumulated emails and text messages. She reads them aloud.

"Wine tasting, cancelled." She flicks to another

message. "Block Island ferry outing? Cancelled." Sitting on the unmade bed then, she flicks through one message after the other. "Concert at The Kate in Old Saybrook? Cancelled! Spa morning at that resort in Westbrook? Done." She looks at Mack still standing at the window. "We're not getting our couple's massage."

"Avery." He sits beside her on the bed. "*I'll* give you a massage."

Avery simply grabs her pillow and throws it at him. "Oh. And that fishing excursion I booked for you?"

"No." Mack sets aside her pillow. "Don't say it."

"Cancelled." She stands and paces the room. "Heck, that's why we rented that snazzy Mustang. So we could have *fun* cruising the coast going to all these events. Now, everything we booked is done." She drops her cell phone on the nightstand and drops with defeat onto the bed. "Done, done, done."

When she looks at Mack beside her, neither says a word. Nothing.

Seconds pass, though, when something else happens.

When their expressions drop, too, as they look at only each other. Then glance away, toward the door. Or the wide-open window. Then back to the other; any smiles, small—if there at all.

∽

The quiet between them lingers after breakfast, even as they walk across the lawn toward the beach. Two sand chairs are looped over Mack's shoulder. His other hand carries an inflated tube. Avery walks a step behind him and carries a canvas tote in one hand, her tube in the other. A beach umbrella is strapped over her shoulder.

"I brought the newspaper for you," she says.

Mack nods, and after a few more steps, stops. "Okay, Mrs. Martinelli. You can call the shots today, since your honeymoon got derailed." He nods to a wide sandy path leading into sweeping dune grasses. "Which path should we take? This one, to the east beach? Or one across the way, to the west beach?"

Avery, wearing a black-and-white striped one-shoulder bathing suit, looks right, trying to spot the other obscure path. Then she looks straight ahead, to a distant view of the water. She does something else, too. Briefly squeezing her eyes shut, she whispers, *Eeny, meeny, miny, mo*. "Okay, Mack," she finally says. "Maybe a beach day is just what we need, after all the craziness of last week. So let's go east."

At its far end, the long sandy beach stops at a grassy peninsula jutting out from the coast. Atop that peninsula, a rambling beach home commands a surrounding view of the sea. But there are only a few other people set up on the sand before that peninsula, so the beach is quiet.

So are Mack and Avery.

Their sand chairs sit at the water's edge, where

gentle waves lap near their feet. Their blue umbrella drops a cool shadow on them. Avery pulls a notepad from her tote and jots some phrases.

"What are you writing?" Mack asks beside her. His deep voice is almost surprising, interrupting the hush between them.

"I have an idea for the window displays at Windmill Plaza. It might be cool to have sandy paths leading from one store window, then continuing to the next, over and over. Like a long trail."

"But you already have your summer displays up."

"I do. And everything's changed now." She writes another line of words. "Everywhere."

"No kidding. My brother texted me."

"Tommy did?"

"Yeah." Mack pulls his cell phone from a pocket in his navy swim trunks. He reads the message on his phone. "*Martinelli Upholstering is nonessential. Business closed. Indefinitely.*"

"Oh, no." Avery sets her pad in her lap. "Your family business, Mack."

He nods, glancing at his phone before dropping it in Avery's tote. "My parents and brother are pretty broken up about it. But it's just not safe out there."

"Windmill Plaza is shuttered, too. They might try curbside pickup for the shops and restaurants. But they're leaving the walkways open so people have a place to go for fresh air outside."

"Not a bad idea."

"That's what I thought," Avery tells him. "So why not have the windows be uplifting in this strange time? All the sandy paths I'm spotting here at Hatchett's Point lead to some surprising beauty, I'm sure. Turn a corner and, *ahh*—a surprise. I'd like that same feeling to come from all the plaza's storefronts—like the walkers are on a winding journey."

She stops talking then, with a glance toward the sandy path leading through the dune grasses. In a moment, she lifts her pen to the pad and writes more. Silently. Mack sits back in his sand chair. Eventually, he peels off his loose tee, grabs his tube and walks into the calm water. He stands there, brushing a hand in the water before sitting in his tube. Giving a few paddles, he slowly drifts out into the Sound.

Avery holds her pen to paper, but stops writing. From behind her tortoise-shell sunglasses, she watches Mack. Finally, she sets aside her notes, tugs down her floppy straw sunhat and brings her tube in the water, too. It takes a while, but she slowly paddles herself out to where he's floating on the rippling water. Their eyes meet, then glance away. They drift apart, then one paddles closer—their hands making small splashes as they do.

At one point, Mack paddles very close to her. He pulls her tube against his, leans over, tips up her sunhat and kisses her cheek. Avery touches his arm before they drift apart again, aimlessly floating and spinning once more.

That night after dinner, they sit at a distressed-white dining room table. Mismatched painted chairs surround it. Seashells fill a wicker basket on the tabletop.

"Argh! Hit!" Mack says.

"I sunk your battleship, Mack Martinelli." Avery starts putting the small plastic cruisers and submarines back into the game's box. "You know what else is sunk? Our honeymoon."

"Oh, don't say that," Mack tells her, collecting their destroyers.

"No, because listen. We were *supposed* to be at a wine tasting tonight at Chamard Vineyard in Clinton. We'd have a nice dinner first, then do some sipping." She gives Mack a small smile as she puts the cover on the Battleship box. "Instead we're playing kids' games out of an old cottage trunk."

Mack leans forward on his elbows. He doesn't say anything until Avery looks at him again. "We can up the ante, Avery. Make these games ... adult. Loser gives that massage?"

Avery shakes her head and moves aside the game. "I'm going to bed."

"What? It's early."

Standing, Avery looks over at Mack. "Do you know what we were supposed to do *tomorrow*?"

"No."

"I'll tell you. Take the ferry to Block Island. It's going to be a perfect summer day and we'd have a nice picnic there, and a bike ride. But now? Well, now I guess we'll just have another beach day."

"Come on." Mack stands and holds out his hand. "Let's go outside and sit on the Adirondack chairs. We'll watch the skies; they're clear tonight. Maybe we'll spot a shooting star. Listen to the waves. See the lights across the Sound. The boat lights shining on the water?"

"*You go,*" Avery whispers. "Go get some salt air, Mack. I'm pretty much feeling overwhelmed ... by everything. I'm just going to sleep."

Mack holds that hand extended and waits until she shakes her head and waves him off. So he scoops up the cottage key from the kitchen counter, lifts his sweatshirt off a chairback and walks outside.

Avery walks, too. First to the bedroom, where she puts on a satin shorts pajama set. She walks to the bathroom next and brushes her teeth. When she's done, she stops in the bathroom doorway and looks toward the bedroom first, then in the other direction. It's dark in the cottage, with no lights on. So she heads to the living room, stops at the window and moves aside the straight curtain. The moon casts just enough light for her to see Mack sitting in an Adirondack chair. He just sits. Minutes pass when he doesn't move, not one bit.

Suddenly, Avery lurches. It's a sob that does it, that wrenches her body. It seems to take hold of her, violently, as more deep sobs surface. They're so harsh, they have her gasp for air. And that seems to frighten her as she glances outside once more. It's as if she fears Mack might hear her. Quickly, she looks around until she spots a large pillow on the sofa. Just as quickly, she lunges for it and presses it to her face, obviously trying to quell the sounds rising from her gut, up through her lungs.

Harder, *harder*, Avery presses her soaking-wet face into that pillow. Her sobs gather all her feelings and fears of the week—that her honeymoon got axed; that her and Mack's family and friends might've been exposed to the virus at their wedding; that she's feeling so vulnerable with her new husband now; that she's afraid of the uncertainty brought on by the pandemic.

By everything.

Still sobbing, Avery sits on that sofa in the pitch-black room. Doubled over, she keeps her face pressed into the now-damp pillow. This goes on for minutes—long minutes—until after several shuddering breaths, she swipes at her tear-streaked face.

And gets frantic.

Frantic enough to run back to the bathroom and splash water on her face, over and over again. After patting it dry, she brushes her sandy blonde hair, pinches her cheeks and takes one last shaky breath. Straightening her satin pajama top and retying the drawstring on her satin shorts, she then walks to the kitchen.

And stops.

And looks around.

Until with a slight tremble, her hands reach for

shortcake and strawberries and whipped cream and a spoon from the drawer and dish off the shelf. Carrying that laden dessert dish, she walks toward the slider outside, but suddenly veers back to the living room and first flicks on the lamp in the window.

Then, as though every feeling has washed out of her with every sob she'd expelled, she simply walks barefoot outside and crosses the damp, dewy lawn.

"I brought you strawberry shortcake," Avery says as she gives the plate to Mack. She sits in the dark, too, in the chair beside his. "I just wanted to say goodnight."

"I'm glad you did." Mack sets his dessert plate on the wide arm of his chair before reaching for Avery's hand.

And that's how they sit. Silent, but holding hands. That lazy moon hanging low over the Sound drops silver light on the water. The air is so damp, you can almost feel the salt of the sea on your skin. Lapping waves down on the beach whisper sweet nothings to fill the silence.

"I left a light on for you." Avery turns in her chair to see the lamplight in the window. It casts a golden glow against the white curtain. "It's pretty, the way the light shines on that trellis of beach roses."

Mack looks back toward the cottage, then resettles in his chair.

"I think it's comforting," Avery practically whispers, "seeing that window lit up. Seeing *any* light shining at night. In the kitchen. Or on a porch." She turns and sits back in her Adirondack chair. Long Island Sound shimmers in the distance. "On a dark night, especially."

"Why's it comforting for you?"

"It's something my parents always do." Avery looks over at Mack. His hair is wavy in the sea damp, and she lightly touches a strand. "So to me, a light left on is a sign. It says ... you're welcome here. Or, or if someone walks out during an argument—no matter how late, no matter how mad or how embarrassed—a light must be left on. No matter what." She pauses then, breathing the salty air. "Oh, it *doesn't* mean anything goes," she says, her voice a little hoarse from her hidden sobs. "It's all about love, that light. It's about coming around to each other, I guess." Again she stops. If it were any lighter outside, or if the moonlight fell on her, Mack might see. Might notice her struggling to quell another sob—a leftover one that she manages to swallow. "*Sometimes?*" she goes on. "Sometimes that light might tell a person nothing more than please come home. That someone's waiting for them."

"It's a nice thought, Avery." Mack watches her in the darkness. "Listen, are you cold in your pajamas? Do you want to wear my sweatshirt?"

Avery shakes her head and stands then. She kisses the top of his head, too. "No, Mack. I'm really tired now. So I'm going in."

"Okay. Love you."

"*Goodnight*," she whispers.

A half hour later, or maybe two hours—it's hard to tell in the night's darkness—Mack walks into their bedroom. Passing the window where Avery left the curtains open, he sits on a chair and takes off his boat shoes. Pale moonlight falls across the wood floor. Mack glances out the window, then walks to the edge of the bed and touches Avery's hair.

"*Avery, are you up?*" He sits on the mattress, moves aside her satin pajama top and leaves a kiss on her shoulder. When he does, she shifts from her side and turns onto her back. Her hand reaches through the darkness and rests on his neck. And pulls him close for a deep kiss.

"*Mack,*" she whispers before sitting up and letting him unbutton her satin top. He lifts it off her shoulders and arms, drawing his fingers along her skin, her sides, her breasts. "*Mack,*" she whispers again. "*I'm so afraid.*"

"*I know,*" he whispers back, kissing her cheek, her closed eyes.

But what seems to surprise him is the way Avery, almost anxiously then, tugs off his sweatshirt—getting a little tangled up in it in the process. But she manages, and gets the rest of his clothes off with more quiet insistence—his tee, his belt and shorts, everything.

Suddenly, in a night that had moved slowly, everything's quick. And urgent.

When Mack presses her down on top of the sheets and pulls off her satin shorts, Avery's kisses grow needy on his body. There's a desperation coming from some aloneness maybe, from the shadows. On top of her now, Mack restrains her arms. And kisses her throat, her face. Their breathing comes fast; the sex does, too. There are no words, no affectionate murmurs between them. There are only sounds—gasps, and grunts, and throaty sighs.

Afterward, they lie side by side on their backs. The sheets are tangled around their bare legs. Their skin perspires. Their chests rise and fall as they catch their breath.

Minutes pass.

Outside the open window beside their bed, the moon rises higher in the black sky. When some of its pale light falls across the bed, across Avery's tear-streaked face, she quietly turns away from Mack and pulls the sheet up close.

three

THE NEXT MORNING, MACK IS up before Avery. Cawing seagulls and the distant breaking waves are the only sounds in the beach cottage. Well, those and the sound of the gurgling coffee maker. A breeze wafts the straight curtains; early rays of sun reach into the rooms. On the teak deck table outside, two plates are set out, as are forks and spoons. Mack sits there, too, idly turning the pages of a magazine.

So he doesn't see Avery walk into the living room, first. Her step is as soft as the lightness of the room. Its white walls are awash in that dappled sunlight; a pale blue throw is tossed over the white sofa. Everything soft in the early light.

Avery stops near the sofa and glances around, as though wondering where Mack is. She stands there wearing a white bikini top and frayed white-denim cutoffs. A long open-front sweater covers it all. The sweater is tan; its loose stitches, airy; the length, just to her thighs. Her blonde hair, side-parted, hangs in a blunt cut to her shoulders.

Barefoot, she crosses the cool wood floor to the kitchen, then stops at the slider to the deck.

Mack looks up from his magazine. "Avery. You're up. And dressed."

"I am."

"What's going on?" Mack asks, turning in his chair.

"Take a walk with me?"

"A walk?"

Avery nods and steps out on the deck. That sea breeze blows a wisp of her hair. "We were so busy these past few months, I never even got to see this cottage. Or have a tour of Hatchett's Point. Show me around?"

"Okay." Mack slowly gets up, as though unsure. Standing there in a white tee and khaki cargo shorts, he pushes in his chair. "How about if we bring our coffee?" he asks.

"Sure, I'll pack my tote," she says, turning back into the cottage.

"Wear your sneakers," he calls out. "Going to do some hiking."

It doesn't take long to get ready. While Mack pours their coffee, Avery tucks a blanket in her tote, and some napkins. Two muffins, too. Right as she's lacing up her sneakers, Mack comes in the kitchen and puts a stuffed brown bag in her tote.

"What's that?" Avery asks, sipping her coffee then.

"You'll see." Mack grabs a navy baseball cap off the

table and puts it on backward. Holding the door open for her, they head out.

———

"You didn't sleep last night," Mack says while crossing the lawn. "After we were together, you were restless."

They walk a few easy steps before Avery answers. "I can't get things out of my mind."

"What's wrong?"

"Nothing. And everything. The pandemic. The headlines. That virus, which is so contagious." She pulls her tortoise-shell sunglasses from her tote and puts them on. "You and I are cushioned from it here. But … what about my parents?"

"What about them?" Mack asks as they take the dune-grass-lined path to the beach.

"My father's high risk. Is it safe for me to see them when we get back? Will we even be with them at the holidays? Everything's in limbo. Then there's your family."

Mack sips his coffee. "*My* family?"

"Yes. And your beautiful upholstering business. It's been in operation for thirty years. Started by your grandfather Maximilian—who you're even named after. The Martinellis have been making people's homes a place of comfort for decades. And all of that might come undone by one virus." Giving a sad shake of her head, she goes on. "You've got a big rent on that building. And bills to pay." Avery steps out of the path and onto the beach. "Oh, I guess I'm just worried *sick* about things. So how can I have a good time and enjoy our honeymoon, with all that's happening?"

"But we'll be okay," Mack insists beside her.

"You don't know that."

"You're right," Mack says, blowing out a long breath. "I really don't."

They cross the beach now, heading toward the peninsula at the far end. They keep to the packed sand at the tideline. To their right, dune grasses sway. To their left, the blueness of Long Island Sound reaches to the horizon. That endless view gives the feel of being stranded on a deserted island.

"Maybe it was all a mistake," Avery suddenly says.

"What was?"

"Getting married the way we did."

Mack stops and turns her toward him. "Avery, come on. Now you're questioning our wedding?"

"No." She gives him a quick smile and pulls the blanket from her tote. "Well, yes. I mean, we saw it all coming—this whole pandemic, and the virus, and how dangerous it is—and we tuned it out. Let's face it, we turned a blind eye and a deaf ear and went on with the show." As she opens the blanket on the sand, gentle waves lap onshore. A sea breeze skimming off the Sound blows her hair. "And maybe that's all our wedding was, Mack," Avery admits while sitting now. "One big show."

Standing there, Mack looks at her, briefly. He lifts his coffee and takes a long sip, saying nothing.

Avery draws up her knees and wraps her arms around them. "Maybe I'm even a little embarrassed that we didn't scale everything back. Or postpone it."

Mack sits beside her on the blanket. "Put off the wedding?" he asks, watching her closely.

She nods. "And take more time. That way, we'd have gotten to know each other better, too. Because let's face it, Mack, our relationship happened so fast! We just met last fall, and the next thing I knew? You swept me off my feet, and I was planning a wedding, and here we are." While saying it, she gives her fingers three quick snaps.

Mack sets aside his coffee cup. Out on the Sound, a pleasure boat passes by, leaving a frothy wake behind it. "All right, then," he reasons. "I hear you. It *was* fast. So … So let's get to know each other more, starting here. Let me tell you about this place that's been a part of my whole life."

"But Mack, what I'm saying—"

"No." He stands then. "You wanted me to show you around before. So you sip your coffee, and *I'll* talk."

―――

In minutes, his voice seems to lull her. As they take a path off the beach and back to the one dirt road, Mack's words tell a story. A story of time, and history, and leisure. He says how the original century-old cottages on the point were modeled after the grand Newport cottages. He and Avery veer off the dirt road here, and there, taking in sights of nature, and sprawling shingled cottages. Back on the road, they circle around *behind* the peninsula and walk the second, western beach.

Two spring-fed ponds, Mack explains. *One on the west, here. One over on the east.*

Small dock, there. Can fish off it. Kayak.

Only nine cottages at Hatchett's Point now. Very intimate place.

Seclusion.

Surrounded by a two-hundred-acre nature preserve.

Privacy.

Fishers Island, he points out once they're back on the east beach and taking in the view of Long Island Sound. *And Plum Island, there.*

"And I want to show you a secret," he says when they reach their blanket on the sand.

Avery's taking off the open-weave sweater she wears over her bathing suit top and denim cutoffs. "A secret?" she asks, folding the cover-up and setting it on the blanket.

He nods. "Grab your tote and follow me."

⁓

Leaving their blanket behind, they walk down the beach again, toward the peninsula jutting out from the coastline. The grassy land and cottage there sit on a raised embankment of boulders.

"Here. Take my hand," Mack says at the ridge of the peninsula. "We'll be walking on the rocks."

Avery places her hand in his.

"Careful," he says, leading her across a few boulders. Their steps are unsteady; they bend and touch the rocks for balance. After the ridge slightly curves, they walk a little more—staying up on the higher, dry boulders. "Okay, stop." Mack reaches into her tote and pulls out two cans of spray paint. With a wry grin, he hitches his head for Avery to follow. A few steps later, he shakes one can and begins spraying a large boulder facing the Sound.

"Mack Martinelli!" she says. "Isn't that graffiti?"

Mack lifts off his backward baseball cap, presses his arm to his forehead, then puts his cap back on. "It's the one place where folks break the rules here. Look." He points to other rocks bearing painted messages.

Avery steps around Mack to see an array of boulders covered in beautifully painted images, and words, and designs. Each painted rock faces the water, visible only to any passing boaters. "This is allowed here? Seaside ... graffiti?"

"It's all a matter of perspective," Mack explains as he continues spraying his chosen boulder. "Plenty of people say graffiti is actually an art form. It tells stories, if you look closely. Like that one." Mack points to one boulder with the initials R + R painted above a date going back decades. "R and R? Those are neighbors of mine here. And that's the very date the couple bought their cottage." He steps further to the left. "There's one, over there. Interesting, no?"

Avery holds back blowing wisps of hair as they stand practically on Long Island Sound. Small waves lap at the peninsula's lower rocks while she reads the painted words. "*The Beach Club*." She looks to Mack. "Some friends, maybe? Coming of age together at the beach?"

"Could be." Mack sets down his paint can and takes her hand as they round a slight curve. "How about that one?"

"*Be wild.*" Avery whispers the words painted on another boulder. "Oh, I love it. And can only *imagine* the story behind it." She considers that graffiti again. "*Be wild.*"

Mack looks long at her, then leads her back to his partially painted rock. There, he gives her a paint can of her own. "Have at it, Mrs. Martinelli."

"Seriously?"

Mack nods.

So while Avery chooses a rock to paint, he picks up his own can and works on his. Occasionally one or the other gives their spray-paint can a shake. They swap cans. There's the slow hiss of the spraying paint outlining, or shading in, or touching up.

When all goes quiet, Mack turns to Avery. She's standing there, brushing back her windblown hair. So he walks over and sees her coastal graffiti. On the palest cream-colored boulder, Avery painted a golden sun rising out of the deep blue sea. Mack looks at her, lifts a hand to her neck and kisses her right there on the boulders. "The sun. I like that," he says, his thumb brushing her cheek, her turquoise stud earring.

When he leads her to his design on a nearby boulder facing the sea, she steps closer and reads it. *Avery + Mack*. The words are surrounded with a wavelike border.

Mack nods to his message. "I gave you top billing," he says.

After lunch, Avery changes into her black-and-white, one-shoulder bathing suit, then sits in the cottage living room and reads a book. Occasionally, she whispers a line of the story as though picturing the scene. *"The kite soars higher and higher against the crystal-blue sky, the bat-kite dipping and bobbing in the air currents."*

In the kitchen, Mack makes a second sandwich for himself. He sits at the table now, finishing off that sandwich along with a bag of potato chips.

"Dump it!" Avery's voice calls out from the living room.

"What?" Mack asks around a mouthful of chips.

"Dump it. Every time you reach into that potato chip bag, it rattles. So annoying! Dump those chips on your plate!"

There's quiet then. Dead silence until that noisy bag gives one last rattle as Mack dumps it. "*Okay, okay,*" he says under his breath. "We never lived together before. You had your apartment, I had the house." He silently counts on his fingers, whispering, "*It's only Tuesday? We've lived together three days.*" With that, he leans back in his chair and calls into the living room, "I'll learn!"

More quiet then. Even Mack's chewing is careful now, and slow. One chip at a time. It's *so* quiet, Avery's voice eventually carries through the cottage.

"*The sun still rises,*" she softly reads, "*and paints a swath of gold across the sea.*"

"You're doing that thing again," Mack calls from the kitchen.

Avery looks up from her book. "What thing? I'm just reading."

"I *know*." Mack gets up from the table and stops in the living room doorway. "You tend to read random lines out loud."

"I do not."

He raises an eyebrow. "The sun still rises, and paints a swath of gold across the sea."

"What?" She looks at the page of her open book. "Well … I just— Are we actually keeping score?" she asks, looking up at him again.

Mack shrugs. He stands there wearing his white tee over navy swim trunks now—obviously ready for a swim at the beach. "We *can* make this interesting," he says, drawing a hand along his unshaven jaw. "Next one who does something annoying has to take a dunk in the Sound?"

"It's a deal, Mack Martinelli." Avery stands and drops her book into her beach tote. "It's a deal."

───

As they emerge from the sandy path through the dune grasses, Avery tips up her straw sunhat and looks back at Mack. "Oh, and one more thing I noticed this morning," she says as they step onto the sunny beach. "You hang the toilet paper wrong. The strip doesn't go *over* the top."

"What?" Mack shifts the umbrella he's holding. "Why not?"

Avery walks across the hot sand and stops near the water. "The toilet paper comes off too easy that way, and unrolls too much. Toilet paper should *always* hang from behind."

Mack stabs the umbrella pole into the sand and swivels it deeper. Opening the umbrella then, he connects the top pole to the bottom. After he moves his sand chair beneath it, he peels off his tee while telling Avery, "And you leave empty bottles and cans for recycling in the dish rack. When you *could* very well walk the *ten* steps and put them in the recycling bin out back."

"They were drying off," Avery explains as she opens her sand chair beside his.

"For twelve hours?"

Then, nothing.

Nothing but settling in.

Nothing but both of them sitting side by side until Mack walks the beach a little and picks up a few seashells. He gives them to her when he sits beneath their umbrella again.

Avery drops them in her tote, grabs her cell phone and takes a scenic shot or two: one, a seagull swooping low over the water; the other, a wide vista of blue sky and sea.

"How about one of us?" Mack asks.

"Okay," she says.

Mack takes the phone, holds it arm's length, and snaps the picture while kissing her cheek at the water's edge.

When Avery sits again, Mack reclines his chair and puts his baseball cap over his face. So Avery pulls her book from her tote and opens the story to where she left off.

There's only the rhythmic splash of lapping waves then. And the muffled voices of a couple walking past and talking softly. The sun beats down from high in the afternoon sky. The salt air itself feels drowsy.

"A wave breaks, hissing up onto the sand at the same time he finally, finally hears his brother's long-awaited voice." As she whispers the line, Avery drags her bookmark beneath the words.

Something else happens, too. Mack sits up and

waggles a finger at her. When he stands, he quickly bends and scoops her up—right off her sand chair. The motion is so abrupt, Avery's straw sunhat flips off her head.

"*No!*" she calls while dropping her book and kicking her legs. "Come on, it just slipped! I won't read out loud again."

"We had a deal, Avery." Mack hoists her up higher in his arms and walks straight into Long Island Sound. He splashes through the cold water and heads out deep.

"You put me down, Mack!" Laughing and kicking, Avery tries to twist out of his hold. "The water's too cold," she pleads. "Don't do it!"

"Deal's a deal." After walking deep enough for the water to reach waist-high, he promptly—and gently—drops Avery into the water, shakes his head and returns to his sand chair beneath the umbrella. Once there, he reclines again and tugs his cap low on his face.

It doesn't take long—a minute, maybe—until Avery makes it out of the water. She's dripping wet, top to bottom. Standing in front of Mack, she spritzes any water from her fingertips right onto his tanned belly. To sweeten her revenge, she bends and squeezes any drops she can from her sodden, soaked hair, too, right onto his chest.

four

EVERYTHING ABOUT THE COTTAGE IS white. The walls, painted. The sofa, upholstered. End tables are painted white, as are dressers. Built-in cupboards? White, too. The cottage interior is all light, and airiness. Then there are the splashes of blue. A blue knitted throw draped over the sofa. A blue lamp. Blue seascapes on the wall. Blue stoneware on the kitchen shelves. And of course, blue skies filling every wide, open window.

So Avery nearly blends in with her lightness. With her sandy hair. With her white tee, knotted over cropped white jeans. The tie-dyed jeans, like the cottage, have vague splashes of pale blue.

Avery's walking through the cottage Wednesday afternoon. Moving from one room to another. One bedroom to another. Again, and again. Living room, to dining room. Down the hall to the spare sewing room. There, fabric samples fill wall shelves. And a sewing machine is set up on a long table. All part of Martinelli Upholstering, no doubt.

You'd think Avery is taking in all the details, and atmosphere, of this old sprawling beach cottage. But you'd be wrong. All you'd have to do is watch how she picks up things and sets them right down. A vase from the distressed-white sideboard. A framed family photograph from a bookshelf. A piece of gold-threaded blue upholstery fabric from a white basket. An unlit lantern from a dresser top. A glass fishing float from a white bowl.

Up and down. Up, and down again without a second look. From one room, to the next. There's a near-manic pitch to her pacing. When she's out of sight, her voice floats through the rooms as she talks into her cell phone now.

"How's Dad doing?" she asks, then pauses. "Do you need anything? Anything I can bring for you when we leave Saturday?" More quiet. "Please be very careful." Another pause, then, "We're okay, Mom. Pretty much holed up here at the cottage, the beach." One more pause. "Sure, I'll tell him you both say hello." A beat of silence. "Love you. See you soon."

Then? Nothing but her footsteps again until Mack calls out, "Was that your parents?"

"Yes," Avery calls back. "They're okay, laying low at home." She walks toward the kitchen. "What do you want to do this afternoon?" she asks. "I don't want to go back on the beach and float in our tubes again."

Mack looks over his shoulder from where he's standing at the open refrigerator. "I'm good hanging out here at the cottage. We can keep it easy, maybe bat around a tennis ball later?"

"I'm not really into tennis." Avery pulls out a chair at the kitchen table. Her hands twist a thread on the blue placemat. "Wish there was somewhere we could go. Get a change of scenery at least."

After grabbing a bottled water, Mack sits at the table, too. "Have anywhere in mind?"

She shakes her head. "Everything is just … *here*. The beach. The dirt road. The peninsula. The ponds. And we've done it all."

"We can take a ride. We rented that Mustang to do some cruising. You game?"

"Places are all closed, though. Mini golf, the Florence Griswold Museum, Niantic Cinema. Where would we even go?"

"Nowhere. Just drive. We'll cruise the beach roads, put the windows down. Listen to some rock and roll." He sips his water, then straightens the loose black tee over his cuffed denim shorts. "Drive."

Their Mustang hums along those winding beach roads. The radio's tuned to an oldies station. The car windows are down, and Avery's hair blows in the wind. She sits back and briefly closes her eyes with a deep breath.

"This is nice," she says, looking over at Mack driving.

"Anything to get away from the news on that TV," he tells her. When he reaches over to clasp Avery's hand, she toys with his braided leather bracelet. "We watched so much of it last night."

"Oh, Mack. My mom said the hospital's setting up a virus tent outside now, for the overflow patients."

"It's not good, what's happening out there," he says, nodding to the street ahead.

"I saw today that the curve on the graph isn't even a curve. It's a line, straight up. And all I'm hearing about is hand-washing, and social distancing, and that we should be wearing masks, Mack." They pass a small shopping center. The doors are closed, the windows dark. "But nothing's open," Avery says.

Mack nods. "I'll check the shed at the cottage. My dad might have masks in there. He sometimes wears them while mowing the lawn, to keep his allergies in check."

Avery says nothing more. Neither does Mack. Driving through Old Lyme, they take a turnoff and pass boutiques, and an old-fashioned ice-cream shoppe. Yellow flowers spill from a rusted milk can on its front sidewalk. The milk can is beside an A-frame sidewalk sign. Chalked across that blackboard is one word: *Closed*.

They drive on. The Old Lyme Library, closed. The candy shop, closed. The museum, closed. The art gallery, shuttered.

"It's like a ghost town," Avery whispers, turning to watch the empty streets. "Like a bomb fell and snuffed all the life."

Still, they keep going, getting back onto the main beach road. Traffic is light—when normally it'd be bumper to bumper in the heart of June. They pass empty bait-and-tackle shops, and a popular garden nursery. Flats of flowers and vegetables cover long tables in its outside lot. Petunias spill from an antique pickup truck used as a planter. The truck's hood is propped open and blossoms of pink and white and lavender fill the engine space. More flowers pour from the truck's open windows.

But nowhere are there people. No one. Anywhere.

In the seaside village of Niantic, it's more of the same. Storefronts and restaurants and the movie theater, all shuttered in the bright afternoon sunlight. No tourists stroll in tees and shorts, sandals on their feet, sunglasses on their faces. The sight is so eerie, Mack reaches forward and shuts off the music.

A few desolate blocks later, they cut their drive short and head back to Hatchett's Point.

"That was worse than the news, actually," Mack says as they drive the winding dirt road to their cottage. "It made the whole pandemic … *real.*"

Avery glances behind the car. A cloud of dust rises from the tires; tall trees enclose the narrow road. "*Where is everybody?*" she whispers. "It's like they're all hiding from that awful virus."

An hour later, Mack emerges from the cottage shed. He blows dust off a box half-filled with disposable masks, then looks for Avery as he crosses the deck. Opening the slider to the kitchen, he stops inside. "Avery?" he calls, then walks through the room. But there's no answer. He sets the masks on the dining room table and checks the front porch. No Avery.

"Avery?" he calls again, walking down the hallway to their bedroom. Clasping the doorframe, he swings into the room—to silence. There's only her cell phone charging on the nightstand. So he returns outside to the deck, hurrying now. "Avery!" He turns to where she sometimes sits in the Adirondack chairs. But she's not there.

Leaving the cottage behind, Mack crosses the lawn to the dune-grass path leading to the beach. By the time he's on the sand, he's trotting. He looks left, then right toward the peninsula. He takes a few steps in that direction, squinting into the sun. But Avery's not on the beach.

"*Shit*," he whispers, cutting through a neighbor's yard off the beach and heading to the dirt road. Once on the road, he looks left, toward the peninsula, then veers right—in the direction of his cottage. The afternoon is quiet in the midday heat. Lazy bumblebees hover over marigolds; the air is steamy. Cars are parked at a few cottages, but no one seems to be outside.

So he keeps walking, sometimes half-trotting, and occasionally glancing behind him. Back at his cottage, he passes the Mustang parked there and goes in the cottage front door. "Avery!" he calls out, but nothing. No greeting, no, *Over here, Mack*. Again, he trots down the hallway, through the bedroom, the sewing room, the kitchen. Dragging a panicked hand along his whiskered face, he goes through the slider out to the deck and stone patio. Shielding his eyes, he looks toward the east pond.

And stops.

Slowly, he takes a few steps in that direction. His hand stays raised, shielding his eyes as he crosses the sloping, large lawn. The pond is way off in the distance, past his family's property, in an open land-preserve area.

There's a rickety old dock there, too, jutting from the wild grasses fringing the pond water. And there's someone sitting on that wooden dock. Someone dressed all in white—from the bottom of her white jeans to the top of her white tee.

Mack runs, stops just before the dock and stands there in the grass. He takes a few quick breaths, looks away, then back at Avery. She sits on the end of the dock. Her back is to him; her bare feet dangle in the water. Beside her on the wooden planks are her flat leather sandals.

"Avery!" he calls. "What are you doing?"

She glances over her shoulder. "Nothing. Just sitting."

Mack walks closer. "I've been looking all over for you."

"After that drive," she says, "I don't know. I really had to think, alone."

Mack lowers his voice as he steps onto the old dock. It shifts beneath his weight. "But you can't just do that."

"Do what?"

"Disappear. On a *whim*." He kicks off his sneakers and sits beside her. "You're my wife, Avery. I was *worried* about you." He reaches for her, touching her hair, brushing the seashell choker around her neck. "*Talk to me.*"

Avery looks at him for a long second, then looks out at the still pond. Dragonflies hover over it; the sun glints like diamonds off the rippling water; beyond, wispy clouds sweep across the sky. "Seeing all the storefronts shuttered on our drive?" she begins. "The empty streets? It makes me feel like *our* lives are shuttered with it all."

"Our *lives*? But they're not."

"No? Before the pandemic, we were busy, Mack. *Go, go*—yes, stupidly, *go*! We had *every* weekend booked. Every family event penciled in. Plane tickets here, day trips there. Baseball games. Movies. Shopping. And now? Now *we* have to stop, too, because of the virus. And … I'm actually thinking maybe we went too fast, all those months. All that whirlwind. We were so smug, thinking we beat the pandemic. We had the big wedding in the nick of time. The party, the cake, the dancing. Like that virus could never touch us." She takes a long breath, then whispers, *"But after driving today, I feel different.* It *can* touch us." She pauses, unmoving except for her feet swishing in the pond water. "I'm really afraid," she finally admits.

"Of what?" Mack asks. The whole time she's talked, he hasn't taken his eyes off of her.

"Of us, Mack. *Us*. This pandemic is making me stop … and *look* at things. At how we've been living."

"So what are you saying?" Mack asks after a thick silence. "If this lockdown happened before our wedding, are you saying you might not have married me?"

"I don't know what I'm saying anymore." The quiet then is so long, you'd think everything's been said. That Avery just brushed off her thoughts. Until she speaks again. "No." She looks at him. "I *do* know."

Mack sits there beside her. Their feet dangle in the still water. The sun beats on their backs.

And they don't touch.

Instead, they devolve. In their looks. Their posture. Their words.

Without the smoke and mirrors of their old, busy-busy life, it's obvious there's nothing to distract them from what they have—or don't have.

Their words are few as they sit there on the dock. Those dragonflies hover close, as though eavesdropping on the argument. Anyone passing by can see the argument, too, in their crossed arms; in the way Avery swipes away tears; in Mack silently shaking his head.

It could seem that the words don't even matter now. All that matters is that the pandemic has delivered them, alone, to each other—to face any undeniable truths, or questions, that being busy could no longer hide.

When they walk back to their cottage, they take the long way. They cut through the path to the beach and walk barefoot at the water's edge. Not that they say much. It's more like they're absorbing what's really happening, said or unsaid. Fears and threats and worries and vulnerabilities—all of it exposed by one virus locking them in place, alone.

Yet the world keeps spinning; the waves keep breaking; the sun moves across the sky.

Once they reach the dirt road, they step back into their sandals and sneakers before walking toward their cottage. Their faces are drawn. Throats are tight around some dark emotion. Tears are fought. On that one packed-dirt road, a worldwide health crisis has drawn a clear line between Mack and Avery.

⁓

"Hey, there's the Martinellis!" a man's voice calls out as they walk the dusty road. "The newlyweds!"

Avery and Mack watch an older couple cautiously

approach and fully stop about twelve feet away. They stand on the edge of their cottage's lawn; their hands clap; their smiles beam.

"Rafe. Rosa," Mack says, stepping forward before catching himself and holding up a hand. "Really good to see you both."

"We saw your engagement in the Hatchett's Point newsletter!" this Rosa says. She wears a sun visor; her sage-green tank top is loose over denim Bermuda shorts. And her happiness is genuine. If she could, if she didn't have to socially distance, anyone could tell she'd rush right over and hug Mack and Avery, both. Her posture is bursting with the desire to do so.

Mack looks back to Avery. "These are my neighbors, Rafe and Rosa." Returning to Avery's side, Mack puts his arm around her and kisses her head. Quietly, he tells her, "*R and R? Painted on the rocks?*"

Avery nods and smiles at the older couple.

"Mrs. Martinelli," Rafe calls out. He wears a cream-colored polo shirt with a windowpane print over brown shorts. "Welcome to our little neighborhood," he says with a wide wave. "So nice to meet you!"

"My better half," Mack tells Rafe and Rosa. "This here's Avery."

Rafe and Rosa inch a foot or two closer. It's as if they can't get enough of seeing pretty Avery, with her blunt-cut shoulder-length sandy hair. And the way she's dressed in that white tee and white, faintly tie-dyed jeans, she could still look like a bride.

"Mack," Rosa says with a shake of her head. "How's the family? And the business?"

"Well, you know. Everything's closed for the time being. But Mom and Dad are doing good. Tommy's keeping them in line while I'm on my honeymoon here," he adds with a wink.

"And Avery!" Rosa clasps her hands in front of her. "What do you do, when you're not busy being a new bride?"

"I'm actually the visual display director at Windmill Plaza."

"Oh?" Rosa asks. "Is that the place with all those quaint colonial-style storefronts? And the cobblestone walkways?"

Avery nods. "Yes. I coordinate all the window displays in those storefronts, to create a visual piece of art—one that tells a cohesive story among the shops."

"How wonderful. I'll have to look closely next time I'm there!" Rosa tells her.

Rafe motions to Mack. "Now how did you two meet, Mack? Online dating?" he asks.

Mack laughs. "No, Rafe. I'm very old-school. I met my beautiful wife when I picked up her dining room chairs last fall."

"You see," Avery adds. "I was getting them reupholstered in time for the holidays."

Mack nods. "I told her Martinelli Upholstering was booked solid and there was only *one* way her order could be squeezed in."

"And how's that?" Rafe asks.

"If she agreed to have dinner with me," Mack explains. "Now here we are—married. So a stroke of fate brought me to my sweetheart."

"Aw, I *love* a special story like that," Rosa declares.

"I couldn't let this one get away." As he says it, Mack squeezes Avery close. And kisses her head again, as though there'd never been an argument between them. As though Avery never doubted their decision to get married. As though they are blissfully in love.

"Please, Avery. Mack. Can you wait there for just a minute?" Rosa holds up a finger and turns to her cottage. "I have something on the porch for you."

Rosa doesn't wait for an answer. Instead, she hurries across her lawn and disappears onto the porch. Meanwhile, Mack talks to Rafe about the pandemic, and asks if he and Rosa have everything they need to safely stay here.

"We do, Mack. We're even ordering our groceries online."

"*Yoo-hoo!*" Rosa is waving and trotting across her front yard now. She holds a large cup in her hand. "Seeing you two like this, so close, well it's really romantic—especially in these scary times. But remember, all you need to get through it is love. You be sure to lean on each other during this lockdown."

"Oh, Rosa, let me assure you," Mack says, keeping his arm looped around Avery's waist. "There's no social distancing between me and the Mrs. Can barely keep six *inches* apart!"

Rosa nudges Rafe to dig into the cup she holds, and suddenly they're tossing rice across the dirt road so that it sprinkles down on Mack and Avery.

"Good luck!" Rafe calls out as the newlyweds walk away.

"Much joy to you both!" Rosa adds, taking another step closer as she tosses the rice at them.

Tosses it just as Mack loosens his hold and drops his arm from around Avery's waist. And puts some space between them. Tosses more rice just as Avery dips her head and swipes at a tear on her face—before turning and giving a wave.

⁓

Back at the cottage, they hardly talk.

Instead, pots clang a little too loudly. And the flatware drawer is opened too abruptly, jangling the forks and knives and spoons. Avery makes a salad and sets the dishes on the teak deck table while Mack takes out a roasted chicken and baked potatoes from the oven.

Still quiet, there's only the tense sound of forks clicking, deck chairs scraping.

Until Avery asks, "What was *that* all about before? With Rafe and Rosa?"

"What was *what* all about?"

"Oh, you know. That over-the-top lovey-dovey act you put on."

"Listen. Rafe and Rosa are good friends of the family. Been our neighbors for years and years, as indicated on their graffiti rock?"

"And your point is …"

"Avery." Mack sets down his fork. "We were in an argument, which they didn't need to know. So I showed them what they wanted to see. Told them what they wanted to hear. Did you see how they lit up?" Mack stabs at a slice of chicken, saying under his breath, *"Maybe I wanted to believe it, too."*

"Mack. You're taking things wrong. The things I said at the pond—"

"That you're not sure you would've married me if this pandemic hit earlier? There's only one way to take that." Mack looks at her for a long second, then stands and brings his plate to the kitchen.

Avery follows after him. "Everything's just so uncertain with the virus. And unknown. And … and dangerous, Mack. Really, *lives* are on the line out there. And I guess that anxiety crept into my thoughts about everything."

Mack rinses his hands at the sink and grabs his baseball cap and car keys from the counter. "Listen," he tells Avery as he puts his cap on backward. "You let me know when you're no longer uncertain. About me." He heads toward the front door then.

"Wait. Where are you going?" Avery asks after him.

"I don't know. Out. Somewhere. Gas up the car." He plucks a mask from his father's half-filled box. "I'll be back later."

The twilight sky is dusky when he walks outside to the packed-lawn driveway. Putting the Mustang in gear, he pulls onto the dirt road—fishtailing the car as he does—his foot too heavy on the gas.

⁓

Problem is, in a pandemic, there's nowhere to go. Nothing to do.

Options are limited—but grocery stores are always one of them. So after Mack drives aimlessly on the deserted, haunted-looking streets, that's where he ends up. Putting on his mask, he grabs a cart and walks up and down each and every store aisle at SaveRite Supermarket. Large adhesive arrows on the floor now indicate the one-way direction shoppers must walk to accommodate social distancing.

He walks slowly, as though he truly needs what being in the store offers: time. Time to think. To breathe deeply. To step away. Every now and then, he reaches for something from the picked-over shelves—a loaf of bread; a can of vegetables; granola bars. By the time he gets to the register, he's got a half-dozen items to ring out.

"How're you doing?" he asks the cashier as he loads his items on the register.

"Okay."

Mack waits, watching the register screen as the cashier rings out his items. When she suddenly stops—

just stops—he looks over at her.

"Sorry," she says, wiping a tear from her cheek.

"Everything all right?" Mack asks.

The cashier shakes her head, then rings the last of his items. "Didn't mean for you to see that. It's just that I've rung out *so* many people today," she explains. "And I'm afraid. The store has no register shields yet. And I have family." Looking up at Mack, her eyes are red-rimmed. She'd been crying much of the day, apparently. "*What if I bring the virus home to them?*" she whispers.

Mack hands her a twenty-dollar bill. "I'm really sorry," he says, then motions that he'll bag the items. "Please, let me." When he's finished, he hoists up the one paper bag and looks again at the cashier. "You take care now."

"You, too." She turns to the next customer.

Leaving the store, he glances back before stepping outside. The parking lot is nearly empty now; the sun, setting. Any random customers give each other wide berth in passing. On the way back to Hatchett's Point, Mack first swings the Mustang into a gas station and tops off the tank. By the time he gets to the dirt road leading to his cottage, the sun's gone down. Shadows are long; the road, dark as his car slowly rumbles along the winding path through the forest.

Once the woods are behind him, though, and his cottage is in sight, his headlights shine on someone familiar. It's Rafe, walking a small dog roadside. Mack slows to a stop and leaves the engine idling as he gets out and talks over the top of the car.

"I knew it was you when I heard that sweet purr," Rafe says, pointing to Mack's low-slung, black sports car.

"Ah, Rafe. Any other time I'd tell you to hop in. I'd give you a spin."

Rafe sadly nods. "I know, my friend. These are strange days, indeed."

"You better get home," Mack tells him. "Mighty dark on this dirt road."

From across the street, Rafe hesitates, pulling his small dog close on the leash. "Why don't you come on over to my place, Mack? Stop by."

"No, that's all right. It's a bad time, with the virus. And you know, you're more at risk, being older."

"Yep. Turned seventy just last month."

Mack nods. "Which is why you have to be careful."

"I am. Always. So you come by and we'll sit outside. Six feet apart."

"You sure?"

"Yes. I'd like to toast your marriage, at the very least." As he says it, he turns toward his cottage and tugs his dog along. "Meet you there," he calls out with a wave.

⁓

By the time Mack pulls into Rafe's driveway, Rafe's got an outdoor light shining on his cornhole court, with a can of beer at either pitcher's box.

"To you and your bride," Rafe calls out as he lifts his beer.

"Cheers," Mack says, walking to his pitching spot and raising his can in the toast.

They spend the next twenty minutes sipping beer and tossing square bags filled with feed corn. Their talk winds from a little about the lockdown, to a lot about the summer. Rafe tells Mack he's doing some painting in his cottage. Mack tells Rafe about his wedding last weekend.

"Perfect weather, Rafe. Couldn't ask for a better day. Church ceremony, followed by a reception in an old historic barn."

Rafe tosses a bag of corn and it slides across the opposite cornhole board, stopping just shy of the hole. "Not sure how to say this. But I couldn't help noticing something earlier," he tells Mack.

"And what's that?"

"Well." Rafe sips from his beer can and steps a little closer. "Things seemed tense with you and Avery. I saw you both walking by my cottage. Both of you, alone—which I didn't mention to Rosa."

"Ah, damn." Mack tosses his corn bag and it slides right off his board. "Sorry you had to—"

"You know how it is, having summered here all your life, Mack. A one-road beach community? Can't *help* but notice the neighbors' secrets."

"It's just that," Mack begins, then stops. Instead, he

takes a long swallow of his beer. "Been crazy busy, recently. So we're feeling stressed," he vaguely explains. "And Avery," he says with a glance in the direction of his cottage down the road, "well, she's plenty worried with all this pandemic news. It has her nervous." He looks closely through the night shadows at his old friend. "Doubting things."

Rafe nods. Nods and picks up a corn bag, which he easily tosses. It slides across his board and drops into the hole. "Would you mind me giving you a piece of advice?"

"No, of course not." Mack stands there waiting—ten feet away—beer can in hand.

Rafe squints over at Mack. "You're young, in your thirties. Just married. Hell, got the world in the palm of your hand. *But* ... you don't have the *livin'* there." Rafe steps closer and drops his voice in the still night. "But I do. And some things take a while to learn, so tonight? Tonight I'll give you a heads-up on one of those life lessons. Save you some heartache, maybe."

"I'm listening, Rafe." Mack tips up his can and finishes his beer.

"In an argument? With your beautiful wife? Just remember—and I can vouch for this. The argument's almost *never* about what it seems to be." He turns up his hands, watching Mack watch him.

"That's it?" Mack asks.

"Probably the most important wisdom I can share." Rafe hitches his head toward the black Mustang parked roadside. "Now go on home, kid. Go be with your Avery."

⁓

The Martinelli cottage is completely dark—except for the lamplight shining in one living room window. The golden illumination comes through the straight white curtains hanging there. Right outside the window, heavy beach roses climb the trellis. The blossoms edging the window glimmer in the lamplight, too.

Mack pulls into the packed-grass driveway curving along beside the cottage—which is where he parks the car. After killing the engine, he sits there and just looks at that one window for several minutes. Beyond the cottage, the moon rises far above Long Island Sound. Crickets chirp; distant waves lap over and over at shore.

But Mack watches only that lamplit window before getting out of the car. Reaching into the backseat then, he lifts out his bag of groceries, crosses the dew-covered lawn and walks inside the quiet cottage.

five

THURSDAY MORNING, MACK WALKS BACK from the beach alone. The air is warm and the sun shines bright as he crosses the backyard from the path. His swim trunks are wet; a towel is slung around his neck; a bunch of wildflowers are in his hand. As he nears the cottage, a noise comes through the open windows. He tips his head, listening, then walks inside through the slider off the deck.

That noise is louder—a thrumming hum, starting and stopping. Hum, stop, more hesitant thrums. It's a repetitive, clicking sound.

Holding those fresh-picked flowers, Mack opens one kitchen cabinet, then another. He lifts out a bowl first, then a too-small crystal vase. All the while, that rhythmic humming continues. After opening a second cabinet, he sets the flowers on the countertop and walks down the cottage hallway. As he does, that clicking hum—start, stop—hesitantly continues, growing louder as he nears the sewing room at the end of the hall.

"Hey. What are you doing?" he asks from the doorway.

Avery looks up from where she sits at the sewing machine. Sunlight streams in the window. Thread spools, and pins, and swatches of fabric cover her workspace. Avery's hands maneuver a piece of that fabric; her foot rests on a foot pedal; a pin cushion is strapped around her wrist. "I'm making masks. Especially for your nice neighbors. The ones who threw rice at us?"

"Rafe and Rosa?"

Avery nods, lowers her head and slowly sews a line of stitches. "I'm using some of your fabric samples from that basket," she says, hitching her head to the large white basket nearby. "Is that okay?" she asks, raising her foot from the pedal to pause her stitching.

"Yeah." Mack steps into the room. "Definitely."

Again, Avery presses the foot pedal. That sewing needle thrums through gold-swirled fabric she's feeding beneath the presser foot. "Any chance you can string some rope between the two shepherds' hooks out front? And attach that sign?" Her stitching pauses as she slides over a hand-drawn cardboard sign reading *FREE for Neighbors*.

"This is really nice of you." Mack picks up the sign. "I didn't know you could sew."

"I can. A little bit." As she says it, Avery stitches the sides of the mask, effectively holding its pleats in place.

Mack watches, then brushes through the fabric

samples on the worktable. There's a denim piece; a bandana-patterned piece; blues and creams and greens. "I was just thinking," he says, picking up a flowered fabric. "If you never had your dining room chairs reupholstered, I'd never have even known you."

Still stitching, Avery asks over the sewing machine's hum, "Do you *really* know me, Mack?"

"What?"

"Do you really know me?" she repeats, still hesitantly stitching.

"Avery." He sets down a fabric sample. "Of course I do."

She stops stitching and pulls her nearly finished gold-swirled mask from beneath the presser foot. "What's my favorite food?"

Standing there in his tee and wet swim trunks, Mack only looks at her.

"As a child," Avery continues, "what did I want to be when I grew up?"

From Mack, again no answer. Just a shifting of his feet, a glance at her hand-drawn sign.

This time, Avery's voice is softer. "What's my biggest fear?"

Mack silently shakes his head with no answer.

Avery sets aside the mask and picks up a length of elastic. But her hands? They suddenly stop moving as she only looks at Mack standing near her table. "*When was I last happy?*" she whispers.

In the silence as he only looks back at her, the cry

of a seagull comes through the windows, its call mournful. "Aren't you happy now?" Mack asks, his voice serious. "With me?"

This time it's Avery who doesn't answer. Doesn't say yes. But doesn't say no, either.

Mack waits a few seconds, then picks up the rope and finished masks and heads out the cottage's front door.

Avery takes a long breath before finishing up with the elastic ear loops. Setting the gold-swirled mask down, she goes to the window and sees Mack outside. He's arranging the shepherds' hooks far enough apart so that all her masks can hang on the strung rope. She watches as he ties on the rope, but she walks away then. Walks out of the room and goes to the kitchen. When she reaches for a glass from the cabinet, she notices the handful of wildflowers strewn on the counter.

"*Oh, Mack*," she whispers as she touches a yellow blossom, a lacy green leaf. Bending to a lower cabinet, she pulls out a ceramic white pitcher and fills it with water. One at a time, she arranges the stems of buttercups and yellow goldenrod, Queen Anne's lace and purple coneflowers. Last, she tucks in the wisps of beach grass and wraps a piece of twine around the pitcher, tying a bow beneath the spout.

⁓

During lunch, Mack asks Avery to join him on the beach afterward.

"It's a hot summer day, and I missed you this morning," he says with a small shrug. "Come with me this afternoon."

So as Avery puts on her bathing suit—this one a black one-piece with mesh inserts—Mack digs around in the shed for an old sand pail.

Now they beachcomb at the water's edge. Avery pulls her straw sunhat low. They walk the length of the beach, all the way to the rocky peninsula and back. Seagulls drift on a salty breeze overhead. A few beach umbrellas throw pockets of shade. Along the sand, Mack veers this way, and that, picking up shells. He rinses them in the sea and drops them in the pail. Avery walks along with her head dipped, keeping her eye on the tideline. She adds smooth beach rocks and pieces of sea glass to the pail. The frosted greens and whites and blues shimmer among the wet seashells. Every now and then, she swishes her fingertips through them, clattering and clicking salty shells.

When they get back to their umbrella, Avery sits on her sand chair in the sun while Mack skims a few flat stones he'd picked up. The stones skip and jump along the water's surface, leaving a spray of the sea behind them. When he walks to their umbrella, he pulls a bottle of sunscreen from her tote and kneels on a big blanket beside her chair.

A minute later, Avery slightly—just slightly—jumps at his touch. Mack's leaning behind her and rubbing the white lotion onto her back, just beneath her neck.

The Beach Cottage

Gently he moves aside her hair, his other hand swirling across her skin. When she leans forward, wrapping her arms around her knees, he rubs lotion lower on her back. His hand moves in slow circles; his touch, soft.

They don't talk. There's only the sound of the sea breeze and the crying seagulls. A pleasure boat motors past, too—one of the very few out on the Sound during this lockdown.

Mack adds a dollop of lotion to his fingertips and starts on Avery's shoulders. As he massages in the sunscreen, he leans in.

"*I'm trying,*" he says, close to her ear.

Was his voice too quiet for her to hear over the lapping waves? They splash at their feet, again and again, the waves leaving behind a frothy silver lace as they retreat.

A minute later, Avery lifts her hand to his on her shoulder and clasps it. "The beach flowers you brought me were beautiful," she says, turning her face toward his. She lifts her hand off his and touches her salty fingers to his scruffy jaw. "We can put them on the table tonight, at dinner."

Later, after taking swims, and sunbathing, and walking the beach once more, they head back to the cottage. Their routine's growing familiar: the late-day showers, and dinner prep, and setting the outdoor table. One does this, the other does that. They sidestep around each other, brush arms, cook. Cabinets are opened; the flatware drawer rummaged through; blue stoneware plates set out; napkins anchored with a salty beach rock; the deck umbrella tilted to block the sun.

Today, Mack lifts a twenty-pound bag of charcoal and pours the briquettes into the grill's grate. When he sets the heavy bag aside, he rolls up the sleeves of his chambray button-down over rust-colored shorts.

"No gas grill here?" Avery asks when she brings plates to the deck table.

"No." Mack picks up the can of lighter fluid and squirts the charcoal pieces, giving them a thorough dousing. "What's good about a charcoal grill is that you have a half hour to kill before the coals are hot." He steps back, setting the lighter fluid on a small patio table while the briquettes soak. "Me and my father like to sit out here and chew the fat." As he says it, Mack tosses a few lit matches on the coals in the grill. "Some of the best talks we've had went down on our old webbed chairs, while we waited for the grill to heat."

"Sounds nice," Avery vaguely says, arranging forks and knives at their dishes.

Mack returns the lighter fluid and bag of charcoal to the shed. When he comes back out, he holds a webbed folding chair in each hand. He opens them on the grass near the smoldering grill. The chairs' faded green-and-white webbing sags; the once-shiny aluminum chair frames are dull and dinged. When he finally sits on a chair, it creaks as he settles in.

"Come on, Mrs. Martinelli," he says to Avery, who's just bringing her pitcher of beach grass and wildflowers to the deck. "Join me."

She stands there in a gray-and-white striped top over frayed khaki shorts. Fresh out of the shower, her damp blonde hair is side-parted; small gold hoops hang from her ears. She looks at Mack for a second, then sets down the bouquet and joins him on the lawn, where she sits in the old chair beside his.

"You asked me something before." Mack pulls a small notepad out of his cargo shorts pocket.

"I did?"

He flips to a page where he'd jotted a few lines. "Yes. Questions." He looks over at her beside him. "When you wondered if I even knew you."

"Mack …"

"No. No, listen. It got me thinking. So I'd like to see if you were right."

"What do you mean?"

"I want to see if I know you or not."

Avery opens her hands, motioning for him to begin.

So as the sun sinks a little lower in the early evening sky, and as a neighbor mows his lawn, and as a robin trills a lonely song from a tree in the yard, Mack searches for the truth.

"You asked if I knew your favorite food," he says, drawing a finger beneath the first question. "Well. There are different ways to interpret that. Your favorite meal? Favorite fruit? Favorite candy? Which is anything chocolate, by the way. But when all is said and done, your favorite food—the one that gets your beautiful hazel eyes to drop closed as you savor the flavor?"

Avery leans on the arm of her webbed chair and props her chin on her hand, all while watching Mack.

"Meatloaf. Your mother's meatloaf, dipped in ketchup. Does it every time. And I fully intend to heavily *bribe* your mother to get that recipe so that your eyes drop closed for me, too."

"*Okay*," Avery whispers with a small smile. "Score one for you."

As the black charcoal briquettes become edged in gray, Mack continues. He glances at the notepad. "When you were a kid, what did you want to be when you grew up?"

"Be careful with that one."

"Oh, I will be. I could guess the typical answers. A teacher, maybe. Or a veterinarian. All kids want to take care of animals. But I think not. Not you." He tips his head and squints at her.

"I'm waiting," Avery quietly says.

Mack leans forward and puts his elbows on his knees. Drops his head, too, before looking at her. "A scientist, of sorts, I'm guessing. Something like a geologist."

"A geologist?" Avery asks. "Why?"

"Well, after a lifetime of summers at Hatchett's Point, I've learned something. It's that people are most themselves by the sea. Something shows in them that isn't revealed elsewhere. That salty sea air pares life down to the basics. And I've been watching you collect sea glass all week. And beach stones, instead of shells. So, that's my guess. You'd want to be a geologist and work with rocks. Maybe on the coast."

"Score two for you," Avery tells him with a nod.

"Seriously? You *really* wanted to be a *geologist*?"

"In a roundabout way. When I was little, I wanted to be a farmer."

"No way. You? A farmer?"

"Mm-hmm. Our town sponsored a Farm Day, and my parents brought me to tour a local farm. We took a hayride into the fields. Sat on a tractor. Plucked a corn cob right off the stalk. But I'm pretty sure it was the pony ride that clinched it for me. I still remember that summer day. Oh, it was so hot. I wore a pink shirt with shorts, little ruffled socks with my sneakers. My hair was in two ponytails. *And*—" she says when he waves her off, "*if* I had a farm, the fields would be surrounded with a *rock* wall, using those New England rocks pulled right from the soil. So, a geologist? Close enough."

"Okay. I'll let you *convince* me I got that one right."

"Can't you picture it, Mack? *Martinelli Farm*."

Mack raises an eyebrow, then flips the page on his notepad. "Next. What's your fear?"

She nods. "Any ideas?"

"I have one, yes. *Fear of the dark*," he says, his voice low in the evening air.

"Why would you guess that?"

Mack reaches over and touches her face. When he does, she takes hold of his fingers and waits for his answer.

"Easy," he says, looking past her, then directly into her eyes. "Your story of leaving a light on did it. After hearing it, well, I know what it means if the light's off."

They're quiet then. Painfully quiet. Avery lets go of his hand, shifts in her chair and looks at the grill. He does, too. The black charcoal is changing to silvery gray.

"Are they ready yet?" Avery asks.

"What?" The way he says it, it's obvious her question wasn't what he expected. He must've expected her to say he'd scored another point. Or correctly guessed her fear.

"The charcoals?" Avery nods to the grill. "Are they ready for cooking?"

"No," Mack says without looking at them. "Next question," he says instead. But he doesn't look at his pad. He only looks at her. Looks at her in such a way, anyone can see she doesn't dare look away. "When were you last happy?"

"Oh, Mack. Maybe that's enough questions. You don't have to try to answer."

"I didn't intend to answer that one," he says as he closes his notepad. That neighbor's lawn mower has stopped so now the sound of distant lapping waves carries to them. "And here's why," Mack explains. But he does something more, too. He reaches over and strokes Avery's arm. "When were you last happy?" he repeats.

She waits, her eyes rimmed with tears.

But Mack? Mack shakes his head. "*Only you can answer that, sweetheart*," he whispers.

⁓

They're settled at the teak deck table now. The sizzling burgers are cooked, the sliced zucchini grilled, and the pre-packaged potato salad set out. When they pour the wine, the sun has sunk low on the horizon, far out over the sea.

"Your turn," Mack says as he bites into a dripping, cheese-and-tomato laden burger.

"For what?" Avery scoops a heavy spoonful of potato salad onto his plate first, then hers.

"Your turn to answer the same questions," Mack says around his food. "About me. Let's see if you know the real Mack Martinelli."

Avery answers them all, and quickly.

"Favorite food, pasta. Any pasta. Spaghetti, lasagna, doesn't matter. If there's pasta on the table, you're smiling."

"Fair enough."

"I *could* even say that's when you were also last happy, whenever you last had pasta. But that's not it."

"It's not?" Mack asks, scooping a forkful of potato

salad and dragging it through ketchup.

"No. Oh, no. You were last happy the second you turned the key in that badass Mustang you rented. Some look came over your face as soon as that engine rumbled."

"Oh, you're good, Avery," he says. "It's a guy thing, you know."

"I figured. And what you wanted to be when you grew up? Another easy one. A baseball player."

Mack sits back and tosses up his hands. "Come on, how'd you know?"

"What else does a kid growing up in an Italian family want to be but a New York Yankee?"

"You got me. One left."

"What do you fear?" Avery scoops up a strip of grilled zucchini. She twirls it around her fork, then looks across the table at Mack. Next to the wildflower pitcher, a candle flickers between them. The moon hangs low over the distant Sound. "I don't know," she admits.

"Aha! Got you, then."

"No. No because here's why. In all these months we've been together, I haven't seen any fear from you. Or heard mention of one." She shrugs and pushes away her plate. "To me?" she asks, then sips her wine. After a second, a second when he sets his fork down and sips his wine, too, she quietly says, *"To me, you've always been fearless."*

The Beach Cottage

When Mack later stands at the sink and soaps off the dishes, Avery brings in their drinking glasses. And comes up behind him. Reaching around his waist, she one-by-one drops the glasses in the soapy water. And takes hold of Mack's hands in the water, too. And entwines her wet fingers with his.

They dry the dishes and put them away. She wipes down the countertop; he sets the pendant lights to dim. Afterward, they sit outside again and light globe candles all around the deck. And kill the wine. Every last drop of it gets emptied into their glasses.

Sipping that wine, Avery turns her deck chair to face the beach off in the distance. The salt air is heavier now, at dusk. The moonlight shines misty on the Sound. Early stars dot the sky with tiny smudges of light.

"Mack," she says.

Instead of answering, he gets up and moves his chair beside hers. That's all. Nothing else.

"I have to tell you something," Avery continues.

"What is it?"

She swirls the last of the wine in her glass, then finishes it. "I honestly couldn't see this the day we drove in here, to Hatchett's Point."

"Couldn't see what?"

"This. The good in all this." She sweeps her arm toward the twilight seaside vista. Toward the moon and stars and mist and deep lavender horizon. "I was too preoccupied trying to keep my week's itinerary straight. This place, what day. Where to the next day? But now?

Now I'm thinking I *know* what this all is. This beach, and your cottage."

"And what's that?"

"A blessing in disguise, Mack." She glances at him beside her, then turns her sights onto the purple horizon meeting the deep blue sea. Starlight shines above. "That's how blessings come, you know. In disguise. Hidden. You have to find them." After a quiet second, she whispers, "*Look for them.*"

Mack says nothing. He simply takes her hand in his while she talks in the evening light.

"This," she goes on. "Sitting here with a bottle of wine. Spending hours sitting outside by the sea. I actually love it. I can *feel* it, in my body. For the first time in a long time, I … slowed … down. I'm a part of the night, and how beautiful is that. I'm aware of all that it is." She looks over at Mack, runs her fingers through his dark, wavy hair. "You said before there was a question only I could answer. And I will, now."

"When were you last happy?" he asks, his voice thick.

Avery nods. "Five minutes ago, when I walked out here with you."

As she says it—almost seeming on cue—someone starts playing a piano. The melody rises into the night like gentle fireflies—shimmering, and floating with lightness.

"That's Mr. Hotchkiss," Mack says, nodding to a neighboring cottage. "Growing up, he gave me and my brother piano lessons. And he wouldn't take any money for them, either."

"Nothing?"

"No. All me and Tommy had to do was mow his lawn once a week, for payment. And what a lawn it is," Mack says, shaking his head. "He got the better end of the deal."

They quiet and just listen to the tune moving through the night. The simple melody that maybe captures their own feelings. Mack stands, then, and tugs her hand. "Dance with me," he says.

"I don't know. People might see, Mack. Our deck lights are on. And some of your neighbors are outside."

"Remember the rock I showed you? That one graffiti rock you loved?"

Avery smiles and stands. "Be wild?"

Mack takes her in his arms. They move from the deck down to the stone patio beyond it. Candlelight shimmers on the deck railings, and tiki torches throw wavering light. Mack holds her close around her waist, and his other hand holds hers against his chest. As they barely sway beneath the night sky, Avery rests her head on his shoulder. Her eyes close as the piano plays on, the melancholy song weaving through the mist.

Still holding her close, Mack presses his face to hers. He hums for a moment, then sings a line of the familiar song playing on the piano, just one line. He sings it softly, close to her ear.

"I once was lost ... but now am found."

Avery pulls back. "Mack," she says as they still slow-dance. "I'm sorry about the things I said. About regretting our wedding, about my doubts. I just really got afraid of the pandemic, and of being here alone, and—"

"*Shh.*" Mack touches her lips. "*Shh*," he says again, then lowers his hand to her neck. "Don't worry, I know." He raises his other hand and cradles her face. "*I know*," he whispers again, then leans in and kisses her. His kiss starts light, their lips just touching.

But when Avery kisses him deeper, there's a breathy sob in that kiss, too. Or a gasp, maybe. One of surprise, of hope, as she reaches around his waist and holds him close. As the lone piano plays on, their kiss plays on, too—the intimacy of it, the touch of it, as much a part of the summer night as the misty sea, itself.

six

THE COTTAGE IS QUIET FRIDAY morning. Quiet and still. Hushed might be a better word. The white sofa with a blue knitted throw in the living room, and the white-painted shelves covered with blue stoneware in the kitchen, the white walls, the white-brick fireplace—all of it hushed. Paused, waiting for the day to begin.

The bedroom is just as hushed. Pale early sunlight shines through the open window. The whisper of distant lapping waves is the only sound. Avery lies on her side in bed, one arm across Mack's chest. Her fingers barely move, stroking his skin.

"Do you know what was on our itinerary today, Mack Martinelli?"

Mack kisses the top of her head. "Doesn't matter," he says, his eyes closed with sleepiness. "All that matters is what's on it now."

"*Which is?*" she murmurs.

Mack slips his arm beneath her and pulls her even

closer. "We're staying right here, beneath the cool sheet."

"*Mmh.*"

"I added a couple of other things to the itinerary, too."

"You did?"

"I did. First, the sea breeze is to come in right there," he says, hitching his head to the open window. "And second? Coffee in a little while."

"In a little while?"

"Yeah." Mack turns and kisses Avery's forehead, her cheeks, her lips. "After this." As he says it, he reaches his hands beneath her satin chemise, gently lifts it off and tosses it aside. Moving on top of her then, he nuzzles her neck, rubs his whiskered face against hers.

Avery smiles, and loops her hands behind his neck. Her fingers tug through his wavy hair; she kisses him slowly, one kiss brief, the next longer. She whispers his name, too, her touch on his shoulders, his bare back, as light as the breeze rising off the distant sea.

"I thought you didn't want to sit on a sand chair for seven days," Mack says on the beach later that morning.

Avery lounges on the low chair beside him. Her seat is partially reclined. Her eyes are closed; her bathing suit still damp after their morning swim; her hair, slicked back. The midmorning sun shines warm on them.

"I'm finding I like sitting on a sand chair, actually,"

she admits, turning to Mack and touching his arm. "I'm learning things about myself, being on lockdown like this."

"Learning things? Like what?"

Avery brings her sand chair back to an upright position. She sits there and looks out at Long Island Sound. The sun drops thousands of sparkles across the rippling blue water. The salty air lifts off the Sound in a light breeze. A brilliant white seagull swoops low against the blue sky. "I'm learning to be in the moment," she answers. "And to appreciate it. To hold it close. To know … it's mine."

"Like this one, now?" Mack asks, tipping his head.

"Yes. And I see something *else* now, just by *being* in the moment."

"Which is …"

"Listen. Do you know that song, *Over the Rainbow*?"

"Absolutely. Judy Garland sings it."

"She does. And in one part, she sings about happy bluebirds flying over the rainbow."

When Avery looks at Mack beside her, he only nods.

"And she questions why she can't, too," Avery goes on.

"Why she can't fly over the rainbow?"

"That's right." Avery pulls her knees close and wraps her arms around them, all while looking out at the sea, and the blue sky streaked with wisps of white clouds. Putting on her straw sunhat, she turns to Mack again. "The thing is?" She quiets, and watches that seagull hover on some salty air current.

"What's the matter?" Mack asks.

Avery shakes her head. "Nothing. It's just that, with the pandemic hitting so hard, and so many people catching the virus—and getting really sick with it—and with errands and every trip out needing the utmost precaution, and with fear and worry defining our days now?" Avery watches that same gull dip low over the blue water. "It's just that I feel like I've done it. Being here, right *here* at Hatchett's Point, during it all. For these fleeting, fleeting days, I'm one of the very few lucky ones who has done it."

Mack leans closer. "Done what?" he asks.

She gives a sad smile and motions to the sea and sky practically surrounding them. Their view of blue is infinite. *"Flown over the rainbow,"* she whispers. "And left everything else behind."

Back in the cottage later, Mack leans into the bathroom. "Dress up," he says as Avery towel-dries her hair after a shower.

"Dress up?" Avery stands there in a short robe and wraps the towel around her head. "For what?"

"I'm taking you out to dinner."

"But nothing's open." When she looks over her shoulder, Mack's gone—walking down the hallway. "Mack?"

"I'm taking you out to the patio," he calls on his way to the bedroom.

"*The patio?*" Avery whispers. And whispers again as she's in the bedroom, too, brushing through the closet.

At the same time, Mack puts on a clean black tee over his rolled-cuff denim shorts. Leather boat shoes next, before he's headed to the kitchen.

Avery decides on a sleeveless navy eyelet dress—fitted on top and tiered below her waist—the eyelet fabric sweeping practically to her ankles. After blow-drying her hair, she dresses while Mack's cooking. And she does it again after putting on her dress, then bending to slip on flat sandals. She whispers, "*The patio?*" That patio is partially visible from the bedroom window, so she gives a look. Outside, a wrought-iron bistro table is set on weathered gray stones; candles are lit on the table; crystal glasses sparkle.

In the kitchen, Mack's pan-frying salmon fillets, adding salt, pepper and a dash of garlic butter. He stirs risotto, too, while heating sliced carrots. He also lifts his navy blazer off a chairback. After putting the jacket on over his denim shorts and tee, he gives a pat to the satin square tucked into the blazer pocket.

All as Avery brushes her sandy blonde hair in a sweeping side part, adds a simple gold chain necklace, then leans close to the mirror to put on her gold bar earrings.

"*The patio?*" she whispers once more, smiling now while walking into the kitchen.

Right as Mack opens the slider and with a slight bow, motions to the stone patio out beyond the deck. "Dinner is served, Avery."

───

After dinner, their plates are moved aside. Wineglasses are nearly empty. On the bistro table, candles glimmer, casting soft shadows. Mack goes inside the cottage for a few minutes. When he returns to the patio, he's carrying a crocheted-lace summer shawl. Holding it open for Avery, he asks, "Take a walk with me?"

It's the twilight hour when they cross the lawn toward the beach. The wild grasses whisper beside them as they move through the sandy path. When they emerge onto the long, dark beach, a low swath of red seems painted right at the horizon as the sun sets.

But there's more light, too. Mack takes Avery's hand so that she follows him. They walk to where two sand chairs are set up beneath a beach umbrella—one strung with *hundreds* of twinkly fairy lights. The strands are wrapped around and around each spoke, casting a golden glow on their sand chairs at the water's edge.

"Oh my gosh! Mack! This is *so* beautiful," Avery says as she lifts her shawl around her shoulders. "When did you ever have a chance to set this up?"

"Let's just say I have some helpful neighbors."

"Rosa and Rafe?"

He nods. "And it looks like they added a little

something extra." Mack pulls a small bottle of wine and two glasses out of a basket. He pours a glass and gives it to Avery.

Avery takes the glass and walks close to the water. The ruffled eyelet tiers of her dress flutter in a salty breeze. Raising a toast to the sea itself, she takes a sip of wine before turning to Mack at the umbrella. "I never told you something—all week long," she says, sitting with him beneath the twinkling lights. "But you need to know, Mack. That I do love you … And I love this place. Your cottage. This view. The salt air."

Mack reaches over and touches her hair. "Breathe it, Avery," he quietly says. "Breathe that salt air. Fill your lungs with it." He does, too, sitting back in his chair and taking a deep breath. Long Island Sound spreads out before them. "You know, you said before that you learned things about yourself this week. And so have I. I realized things I wasn't really certain of before this pandemic crashed into our honeymoon."

"What did you learn, Mack?" Avery's voice is soft. Her touch is, too, on his arm.

"I learned that I'd actually been lonely. For a long time. But I never really *knew* it, not until I met you and saw the difference."

"But you have people in your life. Family, and friends."

"It's not the same. One person changed everything for me. You did, right from the get-go. I felt like I *knew* you the first day I met you last fall. Just by seeing that massive dining room set in your tiny apartment, I knew what was important to you. That your table would one day be filled with good food, people, and talk. And honestly? I wanted a seat at that table, Avery, so badly." He leans close, rests his hand on her face and kisses her there once, then again, beside the sea. "I love you, too."

As the sun drops below the horizon, they sip their wine beneath the twinkling umbrella. On the beach, small waves lap, whispering across the sand.

"It's our last night here, Mack," Avery says. "I'm feeling sentimental right now."

"I know. Me, too."

"It's funny, but when we drove down that dirt road that first day, I wondered how I would *ever* get through the week at this secluded beach." She leans forward, wraps her arms around her bent knees and looks at Mack beside her. "Now I don't know how I'll ever bear to leave tomorrow."

"We can always come back here, to the beach cottage. My family divvies up the weeks all summer."

"It won't be the same, though. It won't be our honeymoon." Avery looks out at the sky over the sea. "So I'm feeling a little blue."

"Yeah. Totally get that," Mack tells her, then takes a swallow of his wine.

"And I guess I'm not alone in that feeling, either. Because look," Avery says, pointing to the peninsula over to the right. The curve of land juts from the coastline on a mighty stone embankment. The windows of the large cottage atop it are aglow with lamplight. But that rocky ledge reaches far out into Long Island Sound.

Mack silently watches the dusky view.

"Do you see it?" Avery asks. "The sky above and the sea below are both the *exact* shade of blue. Midnight blue."

"It's pretty amazing," Mack says. "You wouldn't even be able to distinguish between the two, not without that peninsula separating them."

"No." Sitting in their sand chairs, that view of blue quiets them, until Avery says, "I think that sky and sea are nature's commentary on the world right now." She shakes her head. "Awash in blue."

⁓

They wait for that blue hour to pass before returning to the beach cottage. When they walk through the sandy path, the sky is dark, with a heavy moon just rising. So the night is settled in now; the dune grasses, wispy shadows; the wide lawn, shades of black.

As Avery and Mack cross the dewy grass, the cottage rises dark, too. It's just a sleek shadow itself. All of it, except for that lone living room window edged with beach roses.

"You left the light on," Avery says.

Mack, beside her, only squeezes her hand.

They walk across the sloping yard and go inside. But

it's as if the darkness follows them tonight. There's something haunting about it in the cottage. Without turning on a lamp, Avery slips off Mack's blazer in the bedroom. She stands in front of him then, holds his forearms, stretches up and kisses him. And with the night pressing against the windows, and sifting in through the screens, and winding beneath the closed bedroom door, Avery's touch seems suddenly so necessary. She pulls Mack closer as she backs up and sits on the bed.

"*Avery*," he whispers while she still holds on, lifting off his shirt, unbuckling his belt. The whole time, her hands stay on him—undressing him, embracing him, tracing his face, pulling him down, too, as she lies back on the sheets.

Mack touches her hair while watching her. Kissing her then, he drags a hand along her neck, her throat, her breasts. His hand moves lower, clutching at her eyelet dress and lifting it as he kisses her shoulder, her mouth. It's as though they have to hurry, before the night ends—before the light of morning shines on the day they have to leave.

So before even getting that dress off, Avery whispers for him to hold her. "*Please*," she begs in the darkness as his hand slips beneath her back; as his body covers the length of hers; as her legs rise against his hips.

As they make love in a tangle of clothes and shadows and murmured words.

Moments pass afterward as they lie there, only breathing, in the darkness. But only a few moments before Mack helps Avery slip off her dress. Gently, he lifts it over her head, her shoulders. After dropping it on the floor, he takes her in his arms and they lie there on the bed again. Their words come soft as the night ticks by.

"*Mack.*"

Mack presses his mouth to her hair. In the darkness, his voice asks, "What is it?"

"I feel so safe. Right here," Avery murmurs, tracing a finger across his chest. "At this beach. Tucked away from the world with you." She pushes herself up on an elbow and looks in his eyes. "I'm afraid to go home."

Mack takes a long breath. He tugs her close in his arms and kisses the top of her head. "Who knows what we're even going home to tomorrow."

Minutes barely move. Lazy crickets chirp outside the window. A sea breeze whispers past the curtains. It's as though the two of them have stopped the clock, paused the night.

Avery presses her body against Mack. "How long do you think we'll have to live like this?" she asks in the dark.

"Like what?"

"Under stay-at-home orders. Businesses shuttered. Risk everywhere. Caution in every step we take." Again she lifts herself up, seeking some reassurance from his look, his words. "Everything's changed out there, so quickly."

"Not everything," Mack tells her.

"*What?*" she whispers as he eases her back down onto the mattress.

"Everything hasn't changed," he says, turning on his side. She lies on her side, too, facing him. In the black of night, Mack outlines her jaw, her shoulder. Slow, slow. Traces along her breasts, her hip—his touch unseen in the dark, but assuring. "Because I love you, and that's still the same."

Avery smiles beneath his kiss then. And says no more as he kisses her deeper. Doesn't utter a worry, or a fear, as her mouth opens to his.

As he presses her onto her back, moves on top of her, and cradles her face.

Whispers her name.

Loves her again.

seven

MACK LIES ON HIS SIDE beneath the sheet. The early sun rises, its rays glancing into the bedroom. Avery lies behind him. She lightly touches a lock of his dark, wavy hair. Then, nothing. She does nothing more than watch the rise and fall of his breathing. It's regular, and easy, in his summer sleep. Mack doesn't stir.

Not until Avery leans over and scatters kisses up and down his arm. "Good morning, Mack Martinelli," she softly says.

Mack shifts onto his back then. A smile comes, but his eyes are still closed. Avery props herself up on an elbow and touches his scruffy face, lightly, like the touch of a sea breeze. Moments pass when it seems Mack drifts back into that lull of sleep. Avery still watches him, her fingers touching his hair here, his neck there. She leaves more kisses, these ones on his shoulder. Murmurs, too. Sweet nothings whispered close to his ear.

When Mack opens his eyes again and looks at her,

he reaches over and brushes his fingers across her cheek. "Good morning, Avery," he says, his voice low.

"It *is* good," she agrees, pressing close against him. "Let's make the morning last, Mack, and not pack to leave until *after* lunch."

"Excellent idea," Mack tells her. "We'll grab one last beach morning."

"You read my mind."

"Breakfast outside first?"

Avery shakes her head.

"No?" Mack asks.

"No." She slides a leg over Mack and straddles him on the bed. She bends low, too, and kisses him just as easily as the sweet summer morning. "*This first*," she whispers.

There's something special about a last day.

The last day of school.

Or of being single, maybe.

The last day in a cherished home, before moving on.

The last day of the holidays. Or of summer.

The last day of a vacation.

We stop, in a last day. We hold tight to moments. To looks. To a raised wineglass. To a smile. A touch. We briefly close our eyes and try to capture the memory in our thoughts.

Avery tells Mack all this when they sit on their sand

chairs at the water's edge. Then she drops her own eyes closed with a sad smile, a deep breath of the salt air.

"Come on," Mack says, jumping up from his seat. "Last tube ride?"

Avery nods and puts on her straw sunhat. Together then, they float on Long Island Sound. Anyone can see how Avery's stretching out the morning. Instead of filling it to the brim, she lets the morning fill the hours for them. Languidly, she and Mack drift on the salt water. Anytime a current pulls her tube away, Mack reaches over from his and tugs her back. Gently, the inflated tubes bump and nudge. Facing each other, Avery and Mack entwine their feet beneath the sea. Turn some and hook arms. Lean over and kiss. Give each other lazy spins as the water buoys them.

"I want to show you something," Mack says. He wears his baseball cap pulled low against the sun. His dark, overgrown hair curls out from beneath that cap. And his smile is genuine as he hitches his head. "Follow me."

Together they paddle, their cupped hands dipping into the water, their inflated tubes moving parallel to shore. Occasionally he spins around and waits for Avery to catch up.

"Mack? What are we doing?" she asks, tipping up her straw sunhat.

"You'll see." He reaches out his hand and takes hers, pulling her tube close. "Keep paddling."

As they do, the water raises and lowers them. Gentle

rippling waves slosh at the sides of the tubes. When they near the peninsula jutting into the Sound, Mack paddles out a little deeper, and deeper still. Finally, he stops and idly floats in front of the rocky ledge of boulders framing the peninsula.

"Look," he says when Avery catches up beside him.

She turns her tube to face the rocks. When she does, Mack loops his hand through her tube so that they float side by side. "Our graffiti!" she says, then looks to Mack.

"I wanted you to see it from out here on the water." He nods his head to the spray-painted boulders. "Our messages, for all the world to see. There's mine, *Avery and Mack*. And yours." He points to a pale tan boulder. "The rising sun," he says, then leans close and kisses her face.

"Oh, Mack. *All* the painted rocks are beautiful, every one of them." They paddle closer and drift past years' worth of painted messages, and artwork. Each graffitied boulder—some splashed with the salt of the sea, others dry on higher rocks—tells a story. There are initials in hearts, and painted gulls. Personal dates noting significant events, a peace sign, a painted rowboat, written messages.

"Have a favorite?" Mack asks.

Avery looks at him beside her. "You know it." She reaches for his hand and holds it in the water between them. "*Be wild*," she says, looking at the two simple words boldly painted on a prominent boulder.

Quiet seconds pass when only the small waves lap at their tubes. Seconds when the sun shines warm; when seagulls swoop and cry.

In that seaside lull, Avery looks over at Mack. His face is serious. His dark eyes watch only her.

"Sometimes?" he asks as the two of them drift alone on the sea. "Sometimes the wildest thing you *can* do … is let yourself be loved."

eight

One Month Later

THE CAPE COD-STYLE HOUSE SITS on a shaded front yard. The house's clapboard siding is a warm beige, with wide cream trim framing the multipaned windows and wood-planked front door. A berry-and-twig wreath hangs on that door; a planter of golden marigolds sits on the stoop beside it.

Inside, more wide cream trim edges the taupe walls. Worn throw rugs cover the pine floors. Checkered pillows line the gray sofa. Books are piled on a wood trunk coffee table; a framed wedding photograph stands on the rough-hewn mantel; a black sweatshirt is tossed over the staircase banister.

But it's the dining room that gives it away. That lets anyone know this is Avery and Mack Martinelli's house.

Or rather, it's the dining room *table* that does it. The Queen Anne cherry wood table is oval shaped—and shimmers brownish red. The matching cherry chairs are beautifully upholstered with an olive-and-gold tweed fabric. The shelves in the china hutch hold antique plates and cups. But the sideboard? That is covered, end to end, with recently opened wedding gifts—some still partially wrapped. A retro-style toaster, and framed mirror, and countertop wine caddy, and fringed throw blanket. There's a wood-and-marble cheese board, matching bathrobes, Mr. and Mrs. coffee mugs.

Yet it all comes back to the table. That large dining room table with elegant cabriole legs.

On top of the table are boxes of blank thank-you cards, and address lists, and books of stamps, and a thin silver pen. There's a small stack of written and already-sealed thank-you notes, too. The cursive on the envelopes is flowing and gracious. Amidst it all—the notecards and pen and stamps—is a shallow dish, one filled with smooth beach stones and frosted sea glass pieces and salty seashells. A lacy cardigan is draped over the top of one of the cherry chairs.

Above it all hangs an ornate, dark brass candelabra chandelier.

Around the corner in the kitchen, a faded straw sunhat rests atop a suitcase. The suitcase is set near the cellar door. Leaning against the luggage, there's also a canvas beach tote, its blue fabric sun-faded.

But the kitchen is empty. Dimmed recessed lights shine on the cream-colored cabinets. A few dishes are in the white farm sink. Several envelopes—bills, a couple of late wedding cards—are on the countertop. The simmering coffeepot beside the mail is half full; the pot, steaming.

The kitchen opens to a sunroom, off to the side. Midday sunlight pours in through the walls of windows there. Hydrangea bushes outside line the windowsills. The hydrangeas' blue blossoms edge the view of the quiet summer day.

It's a quiet that fills the house, too, so that a low hum of voices carries throughout the rooms. The voices are serious in tone; the words are few. Those voices come from that sunroom off the kitchen.

"Thanks for coming by, Tommy," one voice says. It's Mack. All the paned windows are open. Mack sits on a straight chair beside one, leaning an arm on the sill as he talks through the screen.

"You doing okay, Mack? I wanted to check on you," Tommy answers from outside in the yard. He's casual-looking; his hair, dark; his clothes—cargo shorts with a tee—comfortable. He's talking through the open window to his brother.

"Hanging in there. But Avery?" Mack pauses and sips from his coffee mug. "It's not good, man."

Tommy steps closer to the window. He takes off his sunglasses and clips them on his T-shirt collar. "I hate to hear this. I thought she was doing better."

"She was." Mack takes a long breath and looks at a wood table at the side wall. Sketches are strewn across it, beside an array of colored pencils. Mack walks over and brushes through the papers. The sketches are rough drawings of storefronts. Mannequins are penciled in here; countryside props drawn, there. Wood cutout trees, and a wishing well, and a steepled chapel, an old-fashioned bicycle, colonial lampposts. A shingled cottage. A path runs through each window scene—the path cobblestone in one, a sidewalk in another, a dirt road in another, a sandy path through beach grass in the last. Each path connects Windmill Plaza's storefront displays.

Mack picks up a sketch and holds it up for his brother standing outside the sunroom. "She thought she had the virus beat, and even started drawing up mocks for her window displays last week," Mack tells him through the screen. "But then that cough came back and she could hardly get a breath. It was damn scary, I'm telling you. I called her doctor for help. The next thing, an ambulance came right away. Avery's been in the hospital three days now."

"Will you go see her?" Tommy asks.

"Can't." Mack sets down Avery's sketch. "No visitors allowed—for *everyone's* safety."

"That's tough, Mack. Have you talked to her?"

"We did a video thing the first day. She was so tired. And you know, they intubated her yesterday."

"So she's not conscious."

"No."

"Shit. Think she'll come out of this all right?"

"Avery's strong, Tommy."

"Yeah." Tommy paces back and forth on the lawn outside the window. "Listen, don't you worry about the business. Dad's filling out the small-business loan paperwork. And we ordered the PPE. A few shields for the reception area. Masks. The works."

"Good. That's good." Mack finishes the last of his coffee and sets down his mug. "Governor's talking about a phased reopening. Eventually."

"We got it covered, Mack. You just be there for Avery. She needs you."

"I know."

"Hey, I left Mom's care package at your front door. Don't forget to bring it in. She made you a lasagna and wrapped it in slices. Said for you to freeze it and make a few meals out of it."

"I will." Mack steps back and drags a hand through his hair.

"Listen. I'm going to get home now. I'll fill Mom and Dad in." Tommy shoves his hands in his shorts pockets and shrugs. "Wish I could come in and just give you a hug, man. Tell you everything will be all right."

"No, Tommy. It's best we keep this distance. Stay safe."

"Okay." Still, Tommy steps closer and drops his voice. "But you let me know if you need anything. *Anything* at all. Anytime."

Mack takes a long breath, glances into the kitchen,

then presses his hand to his forehead.

"What's the matter?" Tommy asks, squinting in at him.

"Listen," Mack says through the screen. "The thing is, okay, I can't stay here right now."

"What?"

"I miss her so much, Tommy. And I mean, what if—"

"Don't say that, Mack. Don't you say it, *or* believe it. You be strong for Avery."

"I'm trying. So I'm going to the beach cottage, Tommy. For a few days, maybe. It's close enough to the hospital."

"The cottage? Why?"

"I don't know. Avery really loved it there, you know? And I just feel like …" Mack turns and looks at the sunroom, and glances in the kitchen. "Like a part of her is there."

"But what if they have to reach you? The doctors, I mean. Or Avery, even."

"They all have my cell. I'll give them the cottage number, too."

"You sure about this?"

Mack looks at Avery's drawings, then back at his brother outside. "We were there at the cottage a month ago, me and Avery. We were happy. So, I don't know." Mack pauses, then tells his brother, "I just want to be near the sea."

Later that day, Mack finally emerges from the shadowed woods of the dirt road. Dust rises beneath his pickup truck's tires. The road ahead is empty. There's only the low afternoon sun shining on green lawns and the distant Sound. Rounding a curve and seeing his family's shingled cottage, Mack pulls his truck into the packed-lawn driveway and sits back with a long breath. It's as though he'd been holding that breath the whole drive here. Finally getting out, he walks around to the truck bed and lifts the duffel he packed with a few changes of clothes.

And looks up when someone must've spotted him and calls out his name.

"Mack! Good to see you," Rafe yells as he and Rosa cross the dirt road.

"Rafe. Rosa," Mack says, putting down his duffel and resettling his baseball cap on his head.

His neighbors stop at the edge of his lawn, keeping a safe distance between themselves and Mack. "Where's Avery?" Rosa asks. "Inside already? I'd *love* to say hello."

Mack glances back at his cottage. "No." He looks at Rosa and turns up his hands. "Avery's not here, Rosa. She's not well, actually."

"She's not?" Rosa takes a step closer. "Mack?"

Mack shakes his head. "Of course you'd have no way of knowing. After our honeymoon, well, she got sick. With that virus."

"No!" Rafe exclaims, right as Rosa gasps a surprised breath.

Mack nods. "She did. Happened about a week after we were home, when she started coughing. And came down with a fever, too. It wasn't good."

"Oh my God," Rafe says. "Mack, we're so sorry. Is she okay?"

"No," Mack tells them. "Avery's not doing too well right now."

When Mack pauses, his friends are silent—but they don't take their eyes off him as they wait for more.

"We thought at first that maybe she caught it at the wedding," Mack goes on. "There were a lot of people there. But we investigated, and all our guests were fine."

"Good, that's good, Mack," Rosa says, her hands clasped close.

"Right. So it wasn't that," Mack assures her. "And when we were here at Hatchett's Point, we were pretty much isolated. Which meant she caught it after we got home. And then with contact tracing we got our answer. Right after our honeymoon, Avery stopped at the post office to pick up our held mail, from when we were away."

Rafe's voice drops. "Oh, no."

Mack nods. "Yeah. The post office followed all safety protocols with social distancing, and mask wearing. But the line to get in was long that morning. And even though only a few people were allowed in at a time, other cases of the virus have been traced back to that same location."

"This is just terrible news," Rosa says.

"We did everything we could then." Mack shakes his head. "Once she got sick, Avery quarantined at home. And I did, too."

"You're okay?" Rafe asks.

"I am. I have no symptoms, and tested for the virus a few times. All the results were negative." Mack takes a long breath. "I think it helped that Avery and I did our best to stay apart, the best we could. And we wore masks, even at home. Then? It seemed like she was improving after a couple of weeks. The fever broke. Her cough stopped."

"That's good, no?" Rosa asks, her voice hopeful.

"We thought so, Rosa. We did. Avery even began writing thank-you cards to our wedding guests. Did some work at home, too. A little bit. But one afternoon, she took a turn for the worse." Mack chokes up then. "I won't go into details, but it happened fast. When her cough suddenly came back, it was debilitating. Avery found it hard to even breathe. An ambulance brought her to the hospital a few days ago."

"I am just *devastated* to hear this, Mack." As she says it, Rosa's eyes fill with tears.

"I know. Me, too. We all are." Mack quiets before going on. "The worst of it is that she was intubated yesterday."

Rafe steps closer. "You mean, she's on a ventilator?"

"She is, Rafe."

"But—" Rosa looks past Mack as though Avery will be coming out the cottage door, maybe. "It's so hard to believe. I just saw her a month ago. Poor, sweet Avery."

Mack picks up his duffel. "I'll be staying here for a while and will let you know how she's doing."

"You can't even go see her at the hospital, can you?" Rafe asks.

"No," Mack answers. "No visitors allowed. The doctors will reach me here."

"Mack." Rafe turns up his hands. "If there's *anything* we can do."

"Thank you, Rafe." Mack gives a wave, picks up a cooler, too, out of his truck and heads inside the cottage.

⸺

Later in the evening, Mack manages to eat a piece of lasagna with a small salad. Alone in the cottage, he washes and dries the blue stoneware plates. As he does, he looks out the kitchen window to the backyard. The sun is going down, leaving long shadows on the green lawn. Mack grabs a dishtowel and dries his hands, then stands at the slider door to the deck.

And breathes. In and out. In and out.

Which gets him panicked, as he no doubt imagines Avery's own struggle. The machine breathing for her now. So he puts a sweatshirt on over his tee and cargo shorts before heading out across the yard toward the beach. His steps are quick as he rushes through the sandy path. The dune grasses rustle in the evening air.

Those sweeping grasses brush against him, and at one point, he swats them back.

By the time he's on the beach, he's winded. So he stops there to get his bearings, looking down the length of the twilight beach. It's empty at this hour.

After a moment, Mack walks, then trots across the sand, over the tideline, straight to the water. The waves are small tonight, lapping again and again. At the water's edge, he kicks off his boat shoes and walks right in. He's clumsy, splashing through the shallows until he's deep enough to scoop up handfuls of water and throw them on his face, his neck—sobbing as he does. He stands there, knee-deep, his face bent into his cupped hands, his shoulders heaving. In time, he lifts one more handful of the sea and splashes his face again, then drags his wet hands through his hair.

Before turning away, he steps deeper into the water and stops to look out at the horizon. The twilight sky is lavender above the dark blue Sound. An undercurrent tugs at his legs. Dipping his fingers into the salt water, Mack lifts them dripping and blesses himself—right there beneath that evening sky.

Mack leaves the beach.

There's no urgency to his steps now. If anyone were to see him, they would see a man depleted. With his shoes hooked onto his fingers, he walks barefoot on the sandy path through the beach grasses, which seem to have stilled. Not one blade moves as fireflies rise from the dunes. When he emerges onto the lawn, the cottage up ahead is dark. It's only a black silhouette against the evening sky. Crossing the sloping lawn, Mack approaches the cottage, steps onto the deck and goes inside through the slider.

The rooms in the cottage are silent. No movement. No voices.

No Avery calling out Mack's name.

Or sewing a mask.

Or setting out a board game with a bottle of wine on the dining room table.

Or reading aloud a line from a book.

Mack stops in the kitchen. Just stops. He takes off his sweatshirt and hangs it on a chairback. His every move echoes in the silent rooms—the sweatshirt zipper clicking on the chair. His keys jangling when he drops them on the counter. He stops again, and only looks around: to the backyard behind him; to the bedrooms down the hall.

But he doesn't go to either place.

No. He goes instead to the cottage living room. In the dark, the furniture becomes mere shadows he walks around. Maybe it's better like this. The white sofa, the white-painted fireplace, the white walls? They might mock him with their memories, with echoes of laughter and talking, if the twilight hour didn't drop some darkness on them.

Mack sits in an armchair near the window. The last light of day is visible through the sheer curtains. The horizon over the distant sea is lined with only a smudge of red. So the sky isn't completely dark with night yet. It holds onto the slightest bit of the day's light.

Sitting there, Mack drops his face in his hands.

Minutes pass when he does nothing more than sit there like that.

Until suddenly, he doesn't.

With a quick breath, he stands. Beside him is a tall lamp on the window table. Mack touches the lampshade. In the dark room, he reaches down and turns on that one light. It's the only light on in the entire cottage. The lamp's illumination casts a glow on the walls, the sofa—just a dim hue.

But more so, that lamp casts its light on the paned window behind those sheer curtains. That one window is golden in the evening now. Mack moves closer and nudges aside the curtain. Outside, wild beach roses from the trellis are caught in the lamplight. Their pink blossoms frame the window edge.

While he stands there looking out, night falls over Long Island Sound. Smudges of stars emerge in the sky. He steps closer to the window for a moment, then lets the curtain drop. When he silently sits, it looks like it's to keep vigil—on the cottage, on the distant beach.

A sound then—just one—breaks the stillness.

It's Mack's voice, as he sits alone in the shadows. "*Avery, please,*" he whispers. Leaning forward in the chair beside the window, he rests his arms on his knees and drops his head. "*Please come home to me.*"

There's a pause, a long one, as though he's listening. And waiting. As he sits there, you'd think the world is waiting, too. The night outside is still. Not a breeze stirs the damp salt air.

Mack lifts his head then, and watches that lamplit cottage window. When he whispers once more, this time his words seem to be his only hope. "*Please. Come home.*"

Next—journey into

THE
SEASIDE SAGA

A book series following a group of
beach friends on the Connecticut shore.

FROM NEW YORK TIMES BESTSELLING AUTHOR
JOANNE DEMAIO

The Seaside Saga

Reading Order

1) Blue Jeans and Coffee Beans
2) The Denim Blue Sea
3) Beach Blues
4) Beach Breeze
5) The Beach Inn
6) Beach Bliss
7) Castaway Cottage
8) Night Beach
9) Little Beach Bungalow
10) Every Summer
11) Salt Air Secrets
12) Stony Point Summer
—And More Seaside Saga Books—

For a complete list of books by *New York Times* bestselling author Joanne DeMaio, visit:

Joannedemaio.com

About the Author

JOANNE DEMAIO is a *New York Times* and *USA Today* bestselling author of contemporary fiction. The novels of her ongoing and groundbreaking Seaside Saga journey with a group of beach friends, much the way a TV series does, continuing with the same cast of characters from book-to-book. In addition, she writes winter novels set in a quaint New England town. Joanne lives with her family in Connecticut.

For a complete list of books and for news on upcoming releases, visit Joanne's website. She also enjoys hearing from readers on Facebook.

Author Website:
Joannedemaio.com

Facebook:
Facebook.com/JoanneDeMaioAuthor

Made in the USA
Monee, IL
12 October 2020